Nate EXPECTATIONS

Also by Tim Federle

Better Nate Than Ever
Five, Six, Seven, Nate!
The Great American Whatever

TIM FEDERLE

Nate

EXPEC-

TATIONS

SIMON & SCHUSTER BOOKS FOR YOUNG READERS

New York London Toronto Sydney New Delhi

SIMON & SCHUSTER BOOKS FOR YOUNG READERS
An imprint of Simon & Schuster Children's Publishing Division
1230 Avenue of the Americas, New York, New York 10020

SIMON & SCHUSTER BOOKS FOR YOUNG READERS
is a trademark of Simon & Schuster, Inc.
For information about special discounts for bulk purchases,
please contact Simon & Schuster Special Sales at 1-866-506-1949
or business@simonandschuster.com.
The Simon & Schuster Speakers Bureau can bring authors to your
live event. For more information or to book an event, contact the
Simon & Schuster Speakers Bureau at 1-866-248-3049 or visit
our website at www.simonspeakers.com.
Jacket design by Krista Vossen
The text for this book was set in Minister Std.
Manufactured in the United States of America / 0818 FFG
First Edition
2 4 6 8 10 9 7 5 3 1
Library of Congress Cataloging-in-Publication Data
Names: Federle, Tim, author.
Title: Nate expectations / Tim Federle.
Description: First edition. | New York : Simon & Schuster Books
for Young Readers, [2018] | Sequel to: Fix, six, seven, Nate! |
Summary: When E.T.: The Musical closes, Nate reluctantly returns
home to begin high school and, with his best friend, Libby, makes a
project of turning Dickens' Great Expectations into a musical.
Identifiers: LCCN 2017046573 | ISBN 9781481404129
(hardcover) | ISBN 9781481404143 (ebook)
Subjects: | CYAC: High schools—Fiction. | Schools—Fiction.
| Musicals—Fiction. | Theater—Fiction. | Friendship—Fiction.
| Gays—Fiction. | Family life—Pennsylvania—Fiction. |
Pennsylvania—Fiction.
Classification: LCC PZ7.F314 Nat 2018 | DDC [Fic]—dc23 LC
record available at https://lccn.loc.gov/2017046573

This book is (very) dedicated to David Gale

Prologue
a.k.a.
What It's Like to Be on Broadway
When You Are Only Fourteen

You know how everyone is required to be nice to you when it's your birthday?

Performing on Broadway when you are only fourteen is a little bit like that—except every day is your birthday, with a hint of Christmas. Not kidding.

See, when you're from Pennsylvania, the act of bursting into song in the middle of a drugstore is not exactly celebrated. And, in fact, it occasionally got me chased out into the parking lot. In the old days.

But on Broadway, they pay you (money!) to burst into song. And if anyone's chasing after you, it's only for your autograph.

(Technically, nobody has ever "chased" me for my "autograph," but I'm talking theoretically, here.)

All the other kids in my cast of *E.T.: The Musical* share the same autobiography, or their own version of it. They were the weirdos too, back in their hometowns.

But if you gather enough weirdos, you become a club, and once you're a club, *you're* the normal kids. It's the most amazing thing.

Here's how it breaks down: One weirdo is just a weirdo, two weirdos is a duet, and three weirdos is suddenly a rapidly expanding girl group. One that generally features one boy (me) who's still got relatively convincing high notes, despite his voice getting lower by the minute.

Anyway, you're not me, of course. (Congrats.) But maybe you understand what I'm getting at. That sometimes all you need to do is change your zip code and ~boom~ your life is good. That sometimes, you have to leave your hometown to finally feel at home.

Maybe this is something you can relate to.

Because maybe, just maybe, on *your* last birthday, the jerk in your homeroom who usually ignores you (or worse) instead became a temporary version of nice. Maybe he mumbled, "Happy birthday, or whatever," when the teacher made everyone sing you the birthday song. And this version of fake, temporary kindness, at the very least, gave you a daylong pass: a cone of safety. Nobody was going to push you into a locker or spit on your shirt—they basically legally can't, because it's your birthday. Who does that on your birthday?

Yeah, these things actually happened to me. Pushing and spitting. Back in Jankburg, PA. On the daily.

But, *also*—yeah: These things are in the past. You know the whole "forgive and forget" principle? I'm happy to forgive—it's easier when the jerks doing the pushing and the spitting are back home, 373 miles away from New York (yes, I've counted). Forgive 'em, sure. But I don't want to forget. And I don't need to.

I sleep better here. I *am* better here.

On Broadway, it's like I've got this protective bubble around me, seven days a week. Every day, it's like your birthday and Christmas morning had a baby. And you never even have to hang on to the gift receipts, because everything just fits.

Not Bitter!!

So . . . some breaking news.

The show didn't get a single Tony Award nomination.

I suppose I should get that out now, in case you think the rest of this is gonna be the enlightened thoughts of a famous person. Just don't want to disappoint you.

E.T.: The Musical did get an Outer Critics Circle Award nomination. For costumes. (Yay.) But, look, if you saw the way the rubber E.T. suit glistens in the spotlight, and how the audience oohs and aahs over the whole cast in alien garb for the curtain call (we tap dance!), you'd nominate us for costumes, too.

Correction. Unless you're a Tony Awards nominator. In which case, you'd think we'd opened several seasons ago. Or never opened at all!

Not bitter.

"Well, this is awkward," one of my dressing room-mates says. We're five floors up, backstage at the Shubert Theater, and nobody's making eye contact. The nominations came out this morning. (Well, other shows' nominations did. Not us!)

"Agreed," I manage to kind of say. I'm actually surprised how emotionally it comes out—I thought I'd gotten all my tears out back at Aunt Heidi's place, in Queens. She handed me a square of toilet paper (she says Kleenex is a waste) and murmured something about how "crying in Queens is redundant." Adults like to talk in poetry, did you know that?

Knock-knock. The "nice" stage manager (Lori, not Ashlee, who hates kids) is at our dressing-room door. Stage managers are like teachers who wear all black, as if they're at a funeral where you're expected to carry a clipboard and hound people about not eating chocolate while in costume. "Hey guys," Lori says, "just . . . checkin' in."

Hoo, boy. This particular stage manager never "just checks in," unless something bad is in the air. (Sometimes literally—recently one of my dressing roommates heated up broccoli in the company micro-wave and didn't put a lid on the Tupperware.)

"Are we in trouble?" I ask, and Lori makes one of those faces you make when you're watching a YouTube of a very old dog trying to hop up on a sofa.

"Of course not," she says.

Oh, boy. It really is bad. Any time an adult is checking in but doesn't have punishment up their sleeve, you know something big is going down.

"I just figured you guys might be a little bummed out," Lori says. "You know, because of the news."

"We know," we all say at once.

Really, though, it's a lack of news. Is it news if you aren't even noticed? I mean, I'm not trying to be self-pitying here—I'm still just a kid from the Midwest who managed to break his way into a Broadway show—but, c'mon. Did we really deserve this? The *New York Times* called us "surprising!" and the *New York Post* said: "See this show, if you dare, while it's still running."

In some circles, those are raves!

We dressing-room boys have been on a group-text chain all day. It started with us sending a bunch of GIFs of former Tony Award–winning actresses tripping while they were walking up to the podium. Classic, harmless boy stuff.

By the third nomination category, though—which we were all live-streaming from the comfort of our own studio apartments—when Elliott's Mom didn't get a Supporting Actress nomination (she literally sings better than anyone on the internet), our group text went quiet. And then it started filling up with all kinds of all-cap SWEAR WORDS that I will leave out here. But you can imagine.

"Okay, well," Lori the stage manager says, trailing off before taking off. "Just doin' my rounds . . ." There are just certain things you can't wrap up with a cheery fortune-cookie response. Not that she doesn't try: "Go out there and tell the story tonight," she says, a moment after leaving us, popping back in and looking unconvinced by her own advice. "Oh, and by the way—this is your half-hour call."

The room is quiet. We'll have an audience in those seats in a half hour. No matter how we feel—and we all have a lot of feelings—we'll have to plaster on some smiles and go put on a show.

I don't think people realize how weird and hard it is to perform on Broadway. It's eight shows a week, two of them matinees, and no matter what's going on in your personal life—like, if you happen to regularly kiss the boy who's playing the lead, and thus all you want to do is stare at him when you're onstage together in the Act One classroom scene—you have to just "tell the story."

That was our assistant director's signature phrase, when he'd come back to check in on the show in the weeks leading up to the Tony nominations.

Correction: to our lack of Tony nominations.

"Just go out there," the assistant director said to us

guys, "and get in the mindset of your character. What does your character *want*? That's your only responsibility. To show the audience what your characters want, and to bring your full, professional conviction to it."

"My character wants to be a vital part of a Tony-nominated hit," I wanted to say. But I've been trained to just nod and write down what adults say. This is a good overall life technique, I've come to learn: Just nod at adults, whether you agree or not. Apparently—this is a shock, but my Aunt Heidi told me—adults "just want to be heard."

Try being fourteen!

Oh, the Tonys! The Tonys, for those who don't know—and if you don't, buckle up, because it's gonna be a lot of this—are like the Oscars of theater. Or as I like to say: The Oscars are the Tonys of film.

"At this evening's performance"—the stage manager announcements are now droning on from our overhead speakers, and they're typically pretty epic—*"the role of Elliott's Mom will be played by Marci Carroll."*

All us boys sit up straight, shook by this news. Marci has only been on once, and only for half an act. It was a few months ago, when our regular Elliott's Mom came down with something mysterious after eating a street hot dog on a "disastrous" (her word) first Tinder date with a handsome banker type who, in her retelling, kept calling *E.T.* a "play" instead of a musical. Which made me feel like *I'd* eaten a bad hot dog. Who are these people? Plays instead of musicals? What's next: calling cast albums "soundtracks"?

I shudder at the memory and put gel in my hair.

Anyway, Marci's on for Elliott's Mom tonight.

"And now people start dropping like flies," says Roberto, my dressing roommate who applies too much eyeliner to be playing a seventh-grade boy in mid-eighties California. "Down, down, down we go."

This kid's been in *three* other Broadway shows. Three! I heard a rumor his real name is Robert and his agent made him add the *o* to "stand out." Who knows.

"Wait, why?" I see my lips saying in the dressing-room mirror. "Why are people gonna start dropping like flies?"

"Because," Roberto-but-really-Robert says at me, like I'm eight, "our show didn't get any nominations. So now everyone's over it, and gonna find new jobs."

I'm not over it.

Roberto puts down his eyeliner pencil and clucks his lips at me as if I'm seven, like I'm aging in reverse.

I'm not over any of it.

My dressing room mirror is covered in opening-night cards that I wedged into its metal frame. There's stuff up there from my parents, but not my older brother, Anthony—who doesn't even call musicals "plays" because he doesn't even acknowledge their existence as a concept. Anyway, I'm seeing the greetings like it's opening night all over again: a card with a kitty who's wearing, like, a Shakespeare hat, from Aunt Heidi. A note from Libby, my best friend from Jankburg, PA, who hand-decorated a Halloween card and drew a red arrow pointing at a skeleton, and signed it: "This is me when you're away." (Dead.)

And also my favorite opening night card of all, from Jordan, the boy I've had this . . . secret thing with, for the last couple months. I guess other boys play video games. Jordan just plays with my feelings. He's got the all-time high score.

"*Fifteen minutes*," comes the overhead announcement.

Jordan didn't sign the card, by the way. He just wrote: "From, you know who!" Because I did, and I do. Or at least I thought I did. His dressing room is two floors away.

Can you ever really get to know a guy if his dressing room is two floors away?

I pull open my drawer and fish around, pushing past the lipstick and homework I ignore equally.

"Nate, let's roll," says one of the child guardians, standing in the doorway. If stage managers are teachers at a funeral, child guardians are babysitters on turbo blast. "Gotta get you to wigs."

I wear a wig in the first scene, but it isn't as fun

as it sounds. They are *hot*, and they are expensive, and every adult in the building will remind you of this twenty-four-six. (We get one day off per week.) Damaging a wig is less forgivable than, like, accidentally breaking the arm of a fellow cast member. Cast members are replaceable. Wigs, no.

"Naaate. Seriously. Move it."

I give the international "just one second" sign to the guardian, because I want to find my green rabbit foot. Jordan gave it to me on opening night, to replace the famous green rabbit foot that I carried with me on my *E.T.* audition, and then lost on my bus ride home.

"We gotta roll now, my dude," says the guardian, who never calls me his dude.

I give up on finding the rabbit foot. I was gonna make a wish on it, an earnest wish.

Something about our show, about me and Jordan, about hoping a lack of Tony nominations doesn't signal a lack of a meaningful future. My dad, a maintenance engineer (janitor), once said the most important thing a man can do is start off on the right foot. Is this the right foot? Moving to New York, and New York telling you, "You know what, we don't want you here either, actually."

"My dude," the guardian says, "you're standing on my foot."

He's right. I am. I guess I stood up to go downstairs

to wigs, and checked my phone to see what people online were saying about our zero (that's 0) Tony nominations, and apparently I stepped on the guardian.

My body's kind of doing its own thing these days. Sue it!

I hope none of this sounds like I'm complaining, by the way.

Not bitter!!

It's just . . . the tricky part about having your dream come true is that then you want to hold on to it. Make a wish on it. Put it on a keychain and check on it, thirty times a day, every time you can't remember if your life is real and if the wish stays yours, or stays true, once it becomes real.

Anyway, if you see my green rabbit foot around, tell it I say hi. I've got a ton of wishes I'm trying to narrow down, and I could use a prop. I like to think of wishes as dreams that just majored in musical theater—but I'm weird. As I'm guessing you've already figured out.

The One Concept That Theater Should Borrow from Sports

There's this moment in our show when the character Elliott has a ten-minute break, near the end of Act One. I know this moment like the back of my heart, because I play Elliott twice a week, at the matinees. I'm okay at it. Not sure I'm great.

"I think this audience hates me," Jordan says, glowing and sweaty, as he and I duck into our secret meeting place, in the back stairwell by the fire exit that isn't up to code—which we only know because we hang out on the fire escape and listen to the taxis honk. "Like, I literally think this audience is out to get me?"

Jordan always thinks the audience hates him. He counts his laughs. Or, lack of laughs, if I'm being honest. Nobody has a better voice than Jordan, but do not give the kid a comedy scene.

"The audience is just, like, subdued because of the

lack of nominations," I say, and he rolls his eyes and fans himself.

I should note here that I'm never sweating in this moment, the way he is. It's a personal point of pride that almost nothing makes me break a sweat unless I walk past a cheap pizza place and don't have dollar bills on me.

"*Subdued*," Jordan says, bopping his eyebrows to make me giggle. "New vocab word?"

I don't giggle. "Uh, you'd know if you did the homework."

I give Jordan a tough time about homework, mostly because he flies through our tutoring assignments with total ease, while I struggle to stay focused on anything that isn't perfecting my autograph. Or turning the homework page into a large origami figure of Patti LuPone. (Look her up. *Very* feisty actress, and though she's won like thirty Tonys, I still consider her underrated.)

Jordan's checking his phone, slurping on his water bottle, seeming his regular upbeat self. It's eerie. He didn't get a Tony nomination. Why isn't he the basket case that I'd be if I were him, and had his perfect blonde hair-eyebrow combo?

"I mean, obviously *not* to be a jerk . . . ," I say, and he goes, "Hmm?" but doesn't look up from his phone. I push ahead as if he's being a good scene partner. "Aren't you, like, upset about not getting a nomination?"

He waves it off. "Nah. My manager forwarded me a whole list of famous stage performances that never got any award recognition. She says it's a badge of honor to be respected but not fawned over." I must be scrunching my face up in disbelief, because Jordan looks up and says, "Don't, you're gonna get wrinkles."

And then we hear the cymbal crash from back inside the theater, which signals the moment the FBI agent characters are searching for E.T., in the painted wooden "woods" behind Elliott's painted wooden "house."

I actually do understand why the set didn't get a nomination, to be honest.

"Oh," I say. "Maybe this audience *does* suck." Because usually at this point they burst into applause—there's this whole moment where E.T. makes a bunch of forest creatures pop out and scare the FBI agents, and it's quite thrilling and unexpected, and the music is pretty and kind of violent. But these people are snoozeroo-silent.

"Told you," Jordan says, but not in the way he usually says it. Usually when he says "told you," which happens a lot these days, he kind of *boops* my nose with his hand. And usually after that, he and I sneak in a quick peck. And then, on instinct, he wipes his mouth against the back of his hand and runs back inside for the end of the act, when Elliott appears in a spotlight and belts a high C.

And I'm left behind. I stay outside, and I don't wipe my mouth on anything, and I try to make our moment last as long as it can before an adult inevitably comes to get me.

But today, when he says "Told you," he says it like he's annoyed. The way my older brother does, when he's right about something stupid and irrelevant, like whether or not the Steelers are going to trade such and such football person for another football person.

You know what would be *one* amazing concept that Broadway could borrow from sports? Trading. Like, I would love *Phantom* to temporarily switch its leads with *Hamilton*. Give that chandelier something to fall for.

"I gotta run and sing a high C in a sec," Jordan says before glancing away from me and at the sky, "and also, I think I feel sprinkles, so you should come in too."

"What if rain is just God crying over how unfair theater is?" I say, in a kind of conspiratorial dream-voice.

Jordan snort-laughs and says, "Nate, even for a drama kid, you are truly dramatic."

We push through the double doors and duck under the sign that says NO ENTRY EVER, STRICTLY ENFORCED, when I've had it up to here (picture me pointing at my shoulder right now) with how casual Jordan is being, and I blurt out: "Why are you in such a good mood? I need somebody to be sad with, and the Lord knows my parents don't get what I'm going through!"

"That's your second God reference in five minutes," Jordan says. "Is this a new thing for you?"

Now, this is the part of the show when the female ensemble runs by us in the upstairs stairwell, as they race downstairs to momentarily sing offstage oohs and aahs as E.T.'s ship glows. It's their tradition to ruffle my hair, like I'm a little kid and not a full teenager who likes to find dark corners to kiss in.

"I mean I was sort of using 'the Lord' figuratively, so."

"Anyway," Jordan says, when the female ensemble has passed and all that's left is the scent of exertion and hairspray. "I'm trying to focus on the positive about all the good stuff happening for me—that's why I'm in such an okay mood."

Obscure. What's he getting at? "Good stuff as in what?"

"I had a callback today for a TV show!" He holds out his arms like I'm supposed to hug him, but instead I attempt a high five that ends with me slapping the wall.

"For what?"

"Don't seem too excited, Nate. Jeez."

"No, I just mean—you usually tell me what you're auditioning for."

Constantly. And this kid books a lot of jobs.

Last month, during one of our ten-minute fire-escape breaks, I ran lines with him for a toothpaste commercial that he was up for.

The role was "Cute Boy." So, ideal for him.

I coached him to focus not on the product but on the impact of the product. "Really savor the fact that, with teeth this white, the concept of shame will be a thing of the past," I believe I said. And he booked it! Obviously, he booked it. (You should see his smile.) Jordan shot the commercial in Vancouver and had to take half a week off from the show. I did three performances in a row as Elliott, and though all the song keys are basically too high for me, I always get double the laughs as Jordan. Fact. Not bragging.

Anyway, you won't see *these* slightly mismatched teeth selling any toothpaste, or gum, or mouth-vicinity products. Not anytime soon. My smile looks like a bookshelf after the kind of earthquake that's bad enough to wake up a baby but doesn't actually kill anyone.

"It's for a really big part."

"What is?"

"The TV show. That I auditioned for. Today." Jordan gives me the exact *Why aren't you listening?* face I always give to adults when I have a really good idea and they're busy looking at their phones. "Like," Jordan says, "I wouldn't say it's the lead, but it's definitely a lead-like character."

Sooo, a supporting character, I believe, is the phrase we use for that. Whatever. Perhaps—but not definitely—I'm just envious I don't have an agent or a manager myself. I'm Nate, the boy who got to Broadway with absolutely no adult support except the general cheer of his actress aunt, who googles herself during *The Bachelor* commercials.

"Jordan!" one of the child wranglers whisper-screams up the stairwell. "Enough with the chitchat. You're on in a minute."

He bounces away. That's the only way to describe it. He takes the stairs two at a time. And because I have the overall sensibility and worry level of a fifty-year-old woman, I say, "Don't twist your ankle."

"Oh, I almost forgot!" he says, both ignoring me and also stopping midway on the stairs. He reaches into his costume jean jacket and pulls out the green rabbit foot. *My* green rabbit foot, from *my* dressing room, for good luck. "I borrowed this for the TV audition. Guess it worked!"

He tosses it in an impossibly high arc and I catch it in an impossible display of athleticism. Move over, sports. I'm coming for you.

"You . . . know where I keep my rabbit foot?" I say,

feeling both known and weirdly violated, and holding the rabbit foot tighter than I mean to. Feeling reunited with one thing that feels like New York to me, the way I associate Jankburg with fried food, and New Jersey with fear.

"Of course I know where you keep your rabbit foot," Jordan says, the wrangler now pulling him away by the wrist. "You're Nate. I know all things Nate."

Another moment where, if we were alone, we'd probably spontaneously kiss, by the way. Not that I keep track of these things.

Jordan takes off, and I hear him hit that high C, and it's perfect, as bright and as piercing and as pinpointed as the light on your phone when you're supposed to be sleeping but can't help checking to see if a cute boy texted you back.

I turn the rabbit foot over in my hand. Something feels off. When I examine it more closely, I see that the cheap gold chain that makes it a keychain has fallen off, somewhere. I don't even use it as a keychain. But something about it broke under Jordan's watch.

"It doesn't even matter," I say out loud, to myself—but then one of the adult female understudies ruffles my head from behind, and says, "*What* doesn't matter?"

And when I turn around, her eyes are watering, and I say, out of nowhere, "Can you believe we got zero nominations?" and she says, "I know! Why is everyone not freaking out about this?!"

Because it's her first Broadway show too, even though she's in her twenties. We are Broadway babies together. Bawling Broadway babies. (I'm not actually bawling, but I'm obsessed with alliteration, e.g., English is my best subject.)

We boo-hoo a little, and I say "Finally" into her sweatshirt, because finally I'm allowed to be my emotional self with someone today, without them *not* kissing me or *not* stealing my keychain or *not* smiling when they say my name out loud. "Finally."

"Totally," she says. Score one for me. (I keep a tally of every time an adult agrees with me. Happens more and more these days.)

This is an adult chorus girl I've barely spoken to the whole run. Here we are, holding on to each other like two old people at a fiftieth anniversary of a tragedy of which they're the sole survivors. I heard that when a cruise ship is sinking following an accident, strangers bond very quickly, and if they survive, they stay bonded for life. Maybe that's this moment. Maybe my career is an iceberg and this lady and I are drinking Diet Cokes on the lido deck.

(I've seen *Titanic* seven hundred times. Can we *talk* about Leonardo DiCaprio's hair?)

I pull away from her sweatshirt and comfort myself

21

with the fact that Leonardo DiCaprio and I have the exact same number of Tony Award nominations.

"You're a sweet kid, Nick," this lady says. Like, she calls me Nick, that's for real. "A real sweetie from day one."

And I don't even correct her. I just go, "*Aww,*" and ask her if she has any gum (she doesn't), and then I go back to my dressing room, 'cause I guess we've got to do Act Two of this thing.

Hey, Adults:
Not Everything Is a Lesson!

The next part happens so fast that it's like when you're trying to be good and not have sweets for a couple days, after the costume department informs you that your costumes are getting "a little snug" (literally, they said this). But then, you sneak in a cookie or three and ~bam~ the diet is over in like twelve seconds.

That's how fast the next part is.

"Heidi! Hey! I thought I was meeting you back at home tonight?"

My aunt is at the stage door after tonight's show, looking like a mom in a TV commercial where one of her kids is home from a war and so they celebrate by making instant coffee.

"Oh, Natey," she says, all weird.

And I go, "What, *what*?!" like maybe my dog,

Feather, died back home, and Heidi has to deliver the news. But it's not that.

It's somehow worse.

Aunt Heidi adjusts a strange "summer scarf" that a lot of ladies seem to be wearing these days. New York is so hot in August that it sometimes feels as if you are one of those molten chocolate desserts with a hard outside and an oozing core.

I'll be honest, I'd kill for chocolate of any temperature right now.

"Stage management called and told me they were going to gather your company, right after the show," Heidi says, confused and overheated, her makeup running the slowest race of all time.

"Wait, should I be inside the theater right now?" I say.

When I turn around to check the rest of the stage-door autographing line, I realize I'm the only actor outside, the only one of us tonight who took some selfies with some superfans. (One guy here has seen *E.T.* so many times, he literally calls me out if I screw up a dance step in the scene in the forest.)

"C'mon," Heidi says, and leads me back around the metal barricades that separate the stage door from the pedestrians.

It's been three whole months of *E.T.* and I still feel like I'm lining up for a rollercoaster every time I walk through the stage door and no adult stops me. I still can't believe this is my life, and that I'm this talented to ride this ride.

"Nate!" one of the child wranglers says, once we get backstage. "We've been looking everywhere for you. Didn't you hear the announcement about the meeting in the theater?"

Nope! Because I never hear announcements, as they're always being made when Jordan and I are hiding from the world. The speakers don't work out on the balcony. And even if they did, when Jordan and I are sneaking in a kiss, none of my other senses function properly. Like literally I can't smell anything, I can't hear anything, I can't even taste anything. It's like my insides are a clock that just clicks so, so loud, and way too fast. Jordan never has to worry about missing an announcement, however; his dresser basically acts as a personal assistant, prepping him for interview requests and filling him in on breaking news. What a life.

"Here we go," Heidi says when we enter the Shubert Theater auditorium to join the rest of my castmates. It's the only theater on Broadway that's got green seats. Put another way: Picture a fancy theater. You see red velvet seats, right? Wrong. *Buzzer sound!* Incorrect. The glorious Shubert Theater is the color of your grandma's weird sherbet recipe that actually tastes amazing.

Anyway, earlier I said this part goes fast, and I guess I'm stalling.

And: ". . . that has forced us to make an extraordinarily difficult decision" is the only part I remember clearly, anyway. It's coming from a producer, standing in front of us, delivering terrible news in her signature expensive clothes.

The whole scene playing out in front of me turns into that one feature on your phone where you can make the camera go really fast and then super slow. Everything's both underwater and on fire. Our director, Dewey, is sitting on the foot of the stage, cradling his head, just like he did when we were in tech rehearsals, when E.T.'s ship kept getting stuck on a corner of the proscenium. I look up at it now, where it still bears evidence of a metal gash that never got fixed before opening night.

Heidi takes my hand and I pull it away like I'm fourteen years old and she doesn't know where that hand has been. Which, let's be honest.

"I'm so sorry your show is closing," she says.

Yeah, in case it isn't clear yet: On Broadway, if your show doesn't get nominated for Best Musical, it becomes one of those noble woodland animals that senses it's going to die and goes and hides behind a log so their family doesn't have to watch.

"I'm just so sorry, buddy."

There's something about the way Heidi says it: not condescendingly, or like she's got any easy way to make it better—like she can't hide the fact that showbiz is tough and being a kid is even tougher—that makes my stomach, which prefers to play the role of a clock, instead play the role of a rollercoaster.

Maybe I'm *not* this talented to ride this ride.

A bunch of other kids are crying, and one of the oldest ladies in the show is shaking her head like she's at her own funeral and offended it wasn't better attended.

Our production stage manager, Roscoe, is *thwapping* his hand against a set of keys on his waistband. But two of the female altos are smirking and rolling their eyes in unison, acting a kind of way I hope I never act: like I'm so used to a Broadway show closing, the only way I can process it is to smirk alongside a battle-scarred friend. I'm not smirking. I'm seeing slivers and flashes and feeling sort of faint.

"Nate," Heidi says. "Earth to Natey. Are you feeling okay?"

That's the precise moment when Jordan catches my eye, and freezes me in his patented freeze-vision. He looks so calm, like this terrible news won't affect his perfect-and-full-of-opportunities life, that I do the thing my dad always does when he's mad the Pirates win. I lash out.

"Don't call me *Natey*," I say to Aunt Heidi, loud, loud enough that when my castmate Genna whips her head around to see why I'm shouting, her hair band comes loose, catapults itself toward my eye, and hits it square in the pupil.

And this is the thing that breaks me.

Not the news that my Broadway debut is coming to a crashing end before I could even get the entire original cast to sign my poster.

It's Genna's dumb hair band, *whapping* my eye with perfect aim.

I am somehow, now, half-blinded in a cab, pretending not to cry, and working on a Popsicle that Heidi instinctively knew we should stop for (Popsicles > Advil, FYI). Mostly, though, I'm silently checking my phone with my one good eye, every two seconds. Maybe my phone's broken, though. Jordan hasn't responded to any of my frowny-face texts or "person dying" GIFs that I've sent in the last ten minutes. Since the news.

"Someday this will be a really interesting chapter in your life," Heidi says, moments before we hit a pothole so hard that my Popsicle gags me.

"Heidi?" I say after recovering, and she goes, "Yes, Nate?"—almost "*Natey*" but not, because even adults can learn if you believe in them.

"Not everything is a lesson and not everything is interesting in retrospect," I say.

I chomp down on my last bite of orange Popsicle, and an ice cream headache rings in my head like a terrible summer song, but I still manage to force out: "Some chapters just suck."

Mourning a Hoagie

Okay, I'm in kind of a mean place tonight, maybe, and hiding in Aunt Heidi's bedroom for some alone time. "I'm like fifty percent sure that Jordan is a . . . psychopath now?"

"See, this has always been my theory."

"I know," I say. "I know."

"Just sayin', diva."

Oh, that's Libby—best friend back home, and currently eating a hoagie on a swing set that's around the corner from her house. We've spent a billion hours there staging various outdoor productions for an appreciative audience of squirrels and/or litter.

"Are you eating a hoagie," I say, turning my phone sideways to see better, "on a swing set?"

"Duh."

We're FaceTiming, but the crickets of Jankburg

are no match for the sirens of New York. Everything is an emergency here.

"So, did you literally sob?" she says between bites. "When they announced that you're closing?"

Heidi and I just finished Indian food (I literally don't know if we even have Indian restaurants in Jankburg!) and I'm completely stuffed, but the sight of Libby's hoagie makes my mouth water, because I'm a monster.

"I didn't cry at the normal part," I say, pausing for another siren to pass, and hearing Heidi turn off the shower and hum a new pop song I'm surprised that she, as a semi-elderly person, even knows. "Like, I didn't cry when the producer said *We're closing the show in a week*. I cried when this girl's hair band hit my eye."

Libby hops off the swing, picks up a handful of sand, and throws it into the wind. It immediately backfires, blows back into her face, and makes her wince-scream.

We laugh.

"I thought that was going to make, like, a beautiful moment of wind art!" she shrieks. "Like, I thought the sand was going to shimmer in the moonlight! I suck at art!"

"That's the problem with wind," I say obscurely, with nowhere to go with it.

"So, you cried because of a cornea injury," Libby says, holding up her sandy sandwich, "the way I'm about to cry because my hoagie is ruined."

"Correct."

Heidi ducks her head into her bedroom, where I'm sitting on the floor practicing my splits. "Is that Libby?" she says, so I turn my phone around for the girls to wave at each other. "Nate!" Heidi says. "I'm in a towel!"

"Puh-lease," Libby says, tossing her hoagie into a trash can. "I'm mourning a hoagie and thus can't even see straight right now. Plus, you have the body of a model."

Heidi rolls her eyes at us (but is, as a Virgo, obsessed with compliments) and calls for her kitty to follow her out.

"So, sorry to state the obvious," Libby says when it's just us again. "But: Please tell me this means you and I will be texting each other during science class in approximately one and a half weeks. Like, please tell me you're basically coming *directly* back home by dawn." Now Libby starts to climb up a metal slide, which proves oddly difficult for her. She abandons it, hops off, and begins walking her scooter home.

"I mean, I dunno." God, I hope not. I love Libby but I love New York, too. Don't make me pick a favorite child. "We'll see what my parents say. I don't really know how I'd afford to stay in New York without the show running . . ."

Libby almost gets hit by a motorcycle and yells "*Merrily!*" at him, short for *Merrily We Roll Along*—our thing where we yell out famous flop musicals instead of swearing. Even though we're old enough to swear now. Like, way old enough.

Also, full disclosure: I don't really do the flop-swear thing anymore, but Libby's still into it, and why would I squash her fun?

"Maybe Jordan's mom would let me crash with them," I say, but I don't mean it, and Libby knows I don't.

She knows it's such a non-starter—that Jordan will stay put here, and that I'll come back to a town that somehow both never knew my name but also hated everything about me—that we change the subject immediately, begin talking about Libby's mom; about how muggy it is in New York right now; about how Libby thinks two of her teachers back home are having an affair because they "have these weird fake fights in the hall between the cafeteria and the science lab."

And the image of those normal halls—the halogen lighting, the dull slam of lockers—makes me wanna barf up my Indian food and go get another Popsicle, maybe give myself such an intentional ice cream headache that I'll be deemed medically unable to attend school at all.

"Nate, one last thing and then I have to boogie, because my phone is about to die and a girl should always have a little power to spare."

"Yes?"

"You seem completely unexcited to come home, which is completely offensive as your oldest friend." I take a breath to offer a retort. "Be quiet, I'm not done—because, I will make it so fun and worth it for you to be home. Seriously! And ever since my mom was declared cancer-free for over a year, she lets me have dessert twice a day. So you can partake. If you wish."

"I wish," I say, and we do our thumbs-up thing at the screen, and the call is over—her batteries run out. Or maybe it's just her patience with me.

Another siren goes off, somewhere down below, on the streets of Queens, just as I'm picturing that piercing Pennsylvania school bell that I've always hated—a bell we don't have on Broadway, where tutoring sessions end if you're needed in an emergency rehearsal. And where, no matter how crappy your day is, a group of a thousand people are going to clap for you at the end of the night.

I mean, you have to admit, it's a pretty good way to be a kid, if you have to be a kid.

Heidi's kitty runs back in from the living room and meows at the sirens.

"Same, kitty," I say, pulling back Heidi's curtains to try and memorize the New York skyline, like someday I might be tested on it. "Same."

Teacher, My Teacher

Somewhere in here I should mention that being tutored for a Broadway show is not anything like a real school, with its funky cafeteria trays and frog dissections.

It isn't an ancient 1960s building with bad acoustics, or a football field that's seven times the size of the school auditorium.

On Broadway, it's a mobile classroom in the basement of a gilded golden theater.

My tutor's name is Savanah. Not "Miss Savanah" or "Mrs. Savanah" or Mrs. Anything. Just Savanah. We'd never call our teachers by their first names in Jankburg, but then, we'd never give our teachers audition tips either. Which I do here, all the time.

Savanah is an actress. Or a used-to-be actress. Or, in her words, a "never-quite-was" actress. Her age is somewhere between seventy and almost-not-alive. She showed me some old videos of her singing, uploaded on grainy YouTube clips. And she could really sing. She can still generate a lot of sound, whenever one of us kids gets rowdy. Man, she can go from zero to shouting in no seconds flat.

But mostly she acts like my favorite kind of grown-up, which is: the kind who wishes they didn't have to be a grown-up, but will occasionally act like one if pushed too hard.

"Well, Nate-o," she says to me, "I suppose this is it. We never quite cracked algebra, you and me"—she leans in close and I can smell her day-old perfume, and citrus mints on her breath—"but you'll never need algebra where you're heading."

She hugs me, and I don't cry because I tell myself, *Don't cry.*

"Where?" I say. "Jankburg? Tell that to my parents."

I'm heading back tomorrow. We close the show today, a single matinee performance, a final Sunday, and then I take the bus one-way in the morning. Even though Heidi said something stupid about how every one-way trip is just a round-trip that hasn't been told so yet.

(Heidi just got a new self-help book for toilet reading, and has started speaking in these kind of generic positivity statements that drive me positively negative.)

But I'm still going to miss the heck out of my aunt, and her futon that's always full of crumbs, and the way she pretends not to hear me sneak out into the living room after lights-out, to watch Netflix on her big screen.

I'm going to miss all of it.

Oh, whoops. I am crying. Right into Savanah's sweater.

"I'm going to screw up your sweater," I say, like an idiot, because how can you screw up a sweater by crying.

"Nate, if I can give you one piece of advice," Savanah says. I swear if she gives me some chipper quote like "Every door closing is a window not closing" or some other B.S., I'm gonna kick a wall or push over a recycling canister. But she doesn't.

"This next time in your life—this going back home—it could truly and royally be terrible," she says.

"O . . . kay?"

"It will seem like a version of forever, these next couple years." Her eyes get glassy. She might just give this speech any time a sensitive boy graduates from one of her shows. "It will be a community of people who probably won't get you, or understand what you've been through . . ."

I sense this could go long, and sit on a chaise in the basement of the theater—just as I hear the front doors open upstairs. Crap. I should be back in my dressing room, saying goodbye to the boys, and blasting vintage Britney Spears songs as a warm-up.

"But even if those kids back home don't get you—even if they look at you like you're a four-foot-tall alien—know that there are people who love you, who will be happy when you're ready to come back. Here, I mean. And know that, even if you can never truly go home again, you can, in fact, enjoy Wichita Falls, in doses."

She attempts a smile that makes her face stall like a computer program that's taking too long to load.

"Um, Wichita? I'm from Jankburg."

"Did I say Wichita?" Savanah says. "How funny! That's where *I'm* from."

I hear the stage manager making a *"Ladies and gentlemen of the company, this is your final half hour"* announcement, and Savanah hands me back a piece of homework that I turned in (late) on the Ottoman Empire. A paper I dashed off so half-heartedly that if it were an actual heart, it would not pump enough blood to keep even a Chihuahua alive.

"An *A*," I say. "You . . . genuinely shouldn't have."

"I know," Savanah says, smiling at her handiwork, the unapologetic lie of a great big A grade, splashed across a paper that's got too many half-researched facts, pulled off Wikipedia. "But you know who doesn't care about grades, Nate?"

"Who?"

She grabs both of my shoulders and shakes me. "Show people, baby. Show people don't care if you went to Harvard. They care if you make 'em smile."

It's awkward, because she's still shaking me, a full ten seconds later, but I appreciate this form of self-help—the kind that's less Buddhist than it is Barbra Streisand.

"I should probably . . . ," I start to say, and she releases me and flings me into a wall like I'm a shark and she meant to catch a catfish.

"—get ready for the last show!" she says, for me. And she kind of pats her helmet-hair of a head, and grins at me. She has lipstick on her teeth and seems so vulnerable that all of a sudden I think, I've got to call my grandma and tell her I love her, sometime.

I don't know what to do. I don't want to go to wigs, because that means it's really over. But we've cried here, and we've half laughed. And she said something odd about how alien and short I am. (I'm not just four feet tall, for the record, jeez.) But I love this lady. And so I just turn around on myself, because Heidi taught me that "goodbyes are just hellos that haven't happened yet."

I push open the door that snakes through the secret passage backstage, and I hear Savanah go, "Nate?"

And I say, "Yes, teacher my teacher?" (Old inside joke; she called me her Nate once.)

And she says, "If I were really doing my job right, I'd have given you a D for that Ottoman Empire paper." Her voice gets dark and ragged, just like how the weather can turn its back on you unexpectedly, without warning, back home in Jankburg. The tornado capital of Pennsylvania. "Charm can get you far in Times Square. But be careful back home."

Parting Gifts

"I'll be back for Thanksgiving," Jordan says, in between swigs of hot tea in his dressing room. "And I think I have a hiatus on the series for Halloween, because the director is, like, very into the 'dark arts,' and is spending time at his second home in New Orleans. So I'll see you back home all the time!"

Jordan swings around in his seat and kind of kicks his legs a couple times. "Nate! Wouldn't it be so cool to have multiple homes someday?"

"Uh, maybe? Sounds expensive. But I mean, sure, if I ever made real money. Or I don't die in high school. In Pennsylvania. Faraway Pennsylvania."

Jordan swirls back around in his chair—that's the only word for it, he's a swirler—and looks at himself in the mirror. "Look, we'll FaceTime a ton and we'll text a million times a day and it's going to be like nothing has changed. Proms-ies." That's how he says "Promise" these days. Everything has an -*ies* on the end. Swears-ies.

I stare at a photo tacked to his dressing room mirror of a selfie he took with Lin-Manuel Miranda and that he had his mom print out in color.

"Well, have a blast on the series. It's like, of *course* they hired you."

Oh, to catch you up: Jordan "got" the TV show. The not-quite-lead role. He's a series regular, and when I asked if his name was going to be in the opening credits, he clucked like I'd suggested we wear roller skates to a Homecoming dance, and said, "No, it's going to be one of those shows that are almost mini-movies, where the names don't come on till the end," and I slapped my forehead theatrically and said, "How could I be so stupid?" and he didn't laugh, he just nodded.

"Well, *here*," I say, and I dangle that rabbit foot he didn't mind borrowing for luck. "A parting gift." I hate romance, but I like gestures.

"For *moi*?" he says, with a pretty good French accent, even though he takes and aces Spanish with *poco* (little) effort.

"Yes, for . . . *ywa*," I say—a joke-attempt at "you" plus "*moi*." It comes out weird. Everything is coming out weird these days. Coming *out* is weird.

"But, don't *you* want this thing?" he says, side-eyeing the rabbit foot like it's, well, a dead animal. "For good luck at regular school?"

"Nah. I've got Libby. She's basically a bodyguard in high-tops."

He takes the keychain from me, and our fingers touch, and I feel like I'm being struck by boy lightning.

I push my hand into his, and squeeze it, and say, "Are we just going to totally stop being Nate and Jordan now?"

"Jordan and *Nate*," he says, double-squeezing my hand back, in the least sweet gesture of all time. "I always get star billing."

"Ha, ha."

He leaps up and fake-punches my arm, and says, "You know what your problem is, Nate?" and I say, "Algebra," and he says, "Good one," and I say, "Thanks," and pick up one of his spare Gatorades, which I decide I want and should have.

The overhead speaker comes on, a stage manager with the annoyed voice of a grocery store employee who has to announce a cleanup in aisle six. "*Nate Foster*," the stage manager says, "*we need you in the boys' room to get ready for our last-ever Act Two—like, now.*"

It dawns on me that I never ran late for anything before I met Jordan.

I pull my hand away from his. The human lightning storm has passed. Or, it's still here, but now it feels like a faint electric current that could actually do real damage to my circuitry, or heart.

"Jordan," I say, and put his spare Gatorade back down. Maybe I don't want it. Maybe I have to stop picking things up just because they're there. "I'm sorry that I always make everything weird, but I'm really going to miss you."

And because I refuse to cry until today's curtain call, I pivot hard and reach for the doorknob. But he stops me.

"Your *problem*, Nate," Jordan says, and then takes such a deep breath that the next part comes out like hot air after a summer storm, "is you take everything too serious."

"Serious*ly*," I say, and I guess I see what he means.

When I'm alone in the hallway outside Jordan's dressing room, I mutter "Anyone can whistle" through my gritted jaw, and attempt (fail) to whistle my way back to the dressing room.

Oh. *Anyone Can Whistle.* Leeeegendary Broadway flop. Our Lord and master Stephen Sondheim's biggest doozy. Ran something like twelve performances—total, in all!

So, yeah. I guess I'm still swearing with flops. Even if I certifiably stink at whistling. And saying goodbye.

The Part Where I Hum "So Long, Farewell" with My Aunt

Basically, there's so much crying, if you watched the farewell scene between me and Aunt Heidi on mute, you'd think one of us was dying and the other one just learned they aren't a matching donor for whichever vital organ the first one needed.

Basically, it's that.

I guess it's just our fractured history that turns this whole thing so weepy. She was a long-lost relative, but then she found me. And I crashed with her during my entire *E.T.* run. And a futon became a bed, and an aunt became a mom.

"I'll be back home for Christmas," Heidi finally manages to announce, through the kind of shake-sobs generally reserved for putting a beloved dog to sleep.

"Then I'll vow not to have a good day until Christmas!" I half say, back.

And then we heave-cry some more, and spontaneously hum "So Long, Farewell," and she manages to hand me a twenty-dollar bill, "just in case you need a *healthy snack* at a rest stop."

The Greyhound driver at Port Authority finally stands up and hollers back at us, "I can't hold this bus in the station any longer. If the lady's staying, she needs to buy a ticket."

Which is Aunt Heidi's cue to smudge away her tears, and slobber-kiss my cheek, and walk past the driver to try and whisper without me hearing, "Take care of that kid."

But I hear it. She's an actress. An actress is technically unable to whisper without her audience hearing it. Even when her audience can't stop crying.

All the Things That Could Go Wrong

Once the bus rockets its way through the Holland Tunnel, I open the Notes app on my phone, to make a list of all the things that could go wrong at my new high school in Jankburg. And all the ways I could fight back, if I wanted to. If I had to.

But after I type THING NUMBER ONE: *It's safe to assume nobody wants me back at all, so I'll just act like I don't want to be back*, somehow I nod off, hard.

Apparently, crying hard is a form of exercise, and leaves you in urgent need of rest. And all I've been *doing* the past week is crying hard, and trying hard too—trying to get Jordan to give me a meaningful goodbye, which never seemed to happen. Believe me, you'd have gotten a lot more Jordan here if there were more to give. There were half pecks, sure, and shoulder punches, and promises of "constant texting while we're apart!!!!" All of which felt about as nutritious as cherry pie for breakfast.

Which, by the way, can be delicious. But isn't exactly a way to build a healthy diet. (I've been trying to eat, like, 20 percent better recently. I'm a freshman now. Freshmen worry about health, I heard somewhere.)

When the overhead lights on this bus flicker back on, *one-two-three*, and wake me up without apologizing, it's not one of those cliché things where I "think I'm in a dream" or "wonder if I'm in a nightmare." I know exactly where the heck I am.

My dad is in the Pittsburgh bus terminal in his nice jeans and a red baseball cap. And my mom is holding a just-for-Nate floral arrangement from her flower shop. And she waves at the bus as it pulls in, but on old instinct I don't wave back.

Maybe because I'm shocked Dad showed up at all.

The bus doors *gush* open, and my left leg is numb from this weird position I was in.

"Here I am," I say like an apology, shaking out my leg. And my mom comments on my height, and asks if I've had anything to eat, and we spend the whole ride home with my dad trying to get "the game" to come in clear on the radio. When I ask who's playing (innocent enough, no?), my dad says it's a vintage game—that it was the Pirates vs. the Orioles, "way back when you were a glimmer in your mom's eye."

I'm surprised anyone would *listen* to sports to begin with, let alone sports that took place in the past. I don't even find sports that are happening in front of you, live, intriguing, and they at least have the chance of something exciting happening, like a Broadway-theme halftime show.

Mom drops Dad off at T.J. O'Malley's on the south side of Jankburg, so he can keep listening to the Pirates vs. the Orioles game, surrounded by fellow guys like him. *Normal* guys like him. That's the only reason he came to pick me up at the bus station, it turns out—so he could catch a ride to the pub.

"Here we are," I say, to no one, when we pull into our rocky driveway.

If my dog, Feather, somehow forgot who I am while I was gone, I will be microwaving my head. Just FYI!

The Most Thoughtful People
I Know

Mom hears me in the bathroom around 2 a.m., possibly on the verge of throwing up.

"Natey?" she says from outside, and I jump to my feet—don't want to look weak or like a kid in front of her. She lets herself in just as I knock my knee into the sink and skip around like the very picture of puny.

She looks exhausted, more tired than I've ever seen her. She looks older and it makes me worry.

"Are you . . . a stress-ball about going back to school tomorrow?" she asks.

"Nah, not really," I lie.

"Okay," she says. She's in the same terry-cloth robe she owned from before I went to New York, and it makes me wish I'd bought her, like, a new one, at somewhere nice, like Saks or Forever 21. "Because—I mean, God knows I was never on Broadway myself, but I know what it's like to worry yourself up before a big day. At a new school and all."

I dig my big toe into the old rug that's so worn-out, it's only got the sopping-up power of a name-brand paper towel my mom would never splurge on. "Nah, I mean, I've faced the *New York Times*, Mom. I'm not worried about a bunch of freshmen."

She grins, and the mere act of grinning makes her wince.

"What is it?"

"My dumb old neck," she says, and I say, "Your neck isn't dumb, or old," and it's the nicest moment we've had in so long that I sit on the bathtub because I feel light-headed.

"Well, I'll put a hot water bottle on your bed, just in case," she says, and I groan and say, "I don't really use those anymore, Mom," but she ignores me and turns around to leave, and I remember how bad we are at goodbyes in Jankburg. In New York you really draw out a goodbye, play it for tears. Here, the scenes have no definite endings.

But you know what? When I'm back in my room ten minutes later, after not puking—even though I think I'm on the verge because of my back-to-school nerves—the hot water bottle greets me like a warm puppy. And I cuddle it all night till it's cold, or I am.

Oh, and Feather remembered me, by the way. Of course she did. Dogs are the smartest, most thoughtful people I know.

Here Comes the Lava

When you are fourteen and have a job that doesn't start until 8 p.m. at night, that means you have two dinners—one at 6-ish, so your chicken fingers (most likely) can settle, and another around 11:30 p.m., sitting on your aunt's futon, shoveling down one of God's many beautiful versions of a potato.

"What do you mean, you don't want O.J. with breakfast?"

That's probably why Mom is so surprised when I'm just sitting here at the kitchen table, "awake" (not awake) three hours earlier than I was just a few days ago. Back when I was a Broadway legend. Just kidding.

"Aunt Heidi taught me not to drink my calories," I say, and I'm scrolling through my phone to catch up with my New York friends. But nobody is up, and everything they sent me came in after 2 a.m., when I was still a wide-eyed worried ball.

Mom hides her tongue in her cheek, and places Saran wrap and a rubber band over my unused O.J. cup, and says, "You didn't have any problem drinking your calories when we got a Frosty at Wendy's last night."

And I say, "Doesn't count, it was my welcome-home Frosty!" which somehow makes her smile.

And then Libby's mom *honk-honks* from out front. And for some reason I check my jeans zipper—an old instinct, like: people won't make fun of me if my zipper's up, as if it's some kind of protective Goddess of Dignity—and then give Mom a quick quarter-kiss on the cheek.

"Try to have fun, or have something, today," Mom says, giving up halfway through. She knows moms are supposed to prattle on about good grades, but she was a C+ student herself, at best, and constantly says that if math were so important, why does she never use geometry to run my grandma's failing floral business?

She stands at the door holding her worn-down robe tight and waving at Libby's mom, who rolls down the window and says, "Nice to see you again, Sherrie," and Mom does one of those "What, looking like this?!" mom-things that are so predictable and reaching for a compliment.

I haven't seen Libby since the first preview of *E.T.*—she came to New York to surprise me, and

I fainted, and it was a whole thing—so she catapults her butt out of the car. They are blasting an early-career Kristin Chenoweth album in there, and Ms. Chenoweth is cracking a joke to a live audience (Kristin Chenoweth is the funniest soprano), right as Libby and I half hug and fully laugh, and bounce up and down.

"I hate school so much!" I say as a surprise greeting, and she goes, "Great to see you too, sailor!"

We sit side by side in the backseat, and Libby's mom comments how she feels like our chauffeur. "Perfect," I go. "Can you take us right to the airport for a trip to New York, then? Don't you, as our chauffeur, technically have to go wherever we ask?"

And I guess I say it all too quickly and sharply because Libby goes, "Pump the brakes, Mr. Manhattan, we don't work for you."

Her mom cranks down the Chenoweth album a bit, when Kristin gets to some kind of aria (it's almost always either too early or too late to enjoy an aria; there's like twenty minutes per day when opera is appropriate), and Libby and I compare the school schedule that I posted on Instagram last night. And speaking of operas, it is nearly tragic that we only have one class together.

"What the heck is physical chemistry anyway?" I say.

Libby's mom almost steers her Ford Windstar into a tree, because she swerves so bad.

Libby types *s-e-x* and then *e-d* into the Notes app of her phone, and holds it up for me. And I whisper, "Why are you saying *sexed*," and she shakes her head at me.

Libby's mom, who is as cool as an adult as you can be and live in Pennsylvania, says, "Sex *ed*, Nate, you two are in sex ed together—though Libby thinks the teacher was actually born before sex was even a concept."

And here's an interesting science fact: A year and a half ago I would have gone completely red-hot and also nervous-chilly at the mention of the word *s-e-x*, like I'm in one of those nature documentaries about lava flowing right into the sea. But today I just bust out laughing. And Libby goes, "Just *wait* till our ancient teacher comes up with all sorts of different words for what things actually are," and I'm reminded how refreshing it is to hang out with a family where everyone is in on the joke. "Last week she called a boob a 'fleshy chest' and three of the boys laughed so hard, one of them fell off his seat and had to go to the nurse."

Whoops, here comes the lava. I'm fire-hot, and I already miss Savanah and New York, where you don't really need sex ed because everyone walks around half-naked backstage. So it's kind of a constant, free anatomy lesson.

"This is worse than airport traffic before a holiday," Libby's mom says as we pull up to the front circle at the high school where Libby has been going for two months without me.

Once, she FaceTimed from the girls' bathroom stalls to show me a hilarious piece of graffiti that spelled out exactly where the principal should stick her old-fashioned values, but otherwise, I haven't been back to this school since my big bro, Anthony, won his last track meet, a couple years back, before going off to Penn State.

"You're gonna do fine," Libby says after she sees me holding my seat belt across my chest like it's a bow, and I may need to protect myself in a recess battle. "People care so much less about petty stuff in high school. Mostly."

"Especially their grades," Libby's mom says, and tilts the mirror down to give Libby a rare mom-warning glance.

"I have a 3.2!" Libby says, undoing her buckle and applying some kind of glitter balm to her cheeks, that I'm pretty sure is meant for your lips— but that's Libby, a visionary. "A 3.2 gets me well on my way toward an arts administration B.A. at Pitt!"

"Oh, are we an arts administrator now?" I go.

"Last week you were a fashion designer."

"Did you miss the 'senator of Pennsylva
of Libby's career planning?" Libby's mom
ing behind a stalled pickup truck with the w
of bumper stickers staring at me like a taun

"Ha and ha and ha—we can all stop ga
on my aspirations," Libby says, and has a p
pulls her socks up a little and then re-adju
to the exact same wiggled-down position.
be pigeonholed. If I wanna be a senator wh
pencil skirts, back up and step off."

She opens the door and her mom
mom-routine of yelling, "Wait till I'm park
Libby ignores her and hops out to the cur
scoot out after her. And that's the first time
at my schedule on my phone, I realize son
missing.

"Libster," I go, and she goes, "Yes, Nib
new nickname that I like quite a lot. "Why,"
my fourth-period arts elective in the cafeteria

Her face goes the color of snow ten
before it's officially sooty. "Oh man, Natey. Y
en't heard, have you?"

Libby's mom rolls down her window, reac
grabs my wrist.

"They tore down the auditorium, Nate,"
mom says, simultaneously turning off the

Chenoweth album altogether. "All the arts courses are being slowly replaced with 'practical electives.'"

To a theater person, an auditorium is a church. You look for them wherever you go. They mean safety.

To a theater person, placing "the arts" in the cafeteria automatically makes it dinner theater. And dinner theater is not Broadway.

I jiggle my hand away harder than I mean to, and it flings Libby's mom's wrist into the side of the window, and I can tell it hurts a little, but she preemptively moms me by going, "It's fine."

"They're basically chopping out the arts," Libby says, undoing a side braid that she side-braided in the car, three stops back in traffic. Rethinking her whole look. "But I've become the pied piper of closet theater kids, since I'm the girl who went to New York to see you in *E.T.*—so just stick with me. We've got a whole underground society of dorks here. You'll be the king of dork mountain."

That's when, a hundred yards behind Libby, I see the bulldozer parked outside the Gene Kelly Auditorium, where half the roof missing, and a dozen pigeons are hanging out on a jagged, exposed wooden frame.

"They're replacing the theater with a lacrosse field," she says, putting her hand on my shoulder. "As in: This joint is gonna have a football field *and* a lacrosse field, plus the gym. But no theater. So. Yeah."

I don't say anything. My knuckles sting from flinging them into the window.

"Nate," Libby goes, "say something." The cars behind Libby's mom start *toot-toot*ing, and I still don't say anything. I just tear into my bookbag, and pull out some emergency beef jerky to start my day right.

That's another thing my aunt taught me: Don't drink your calories, but do build your energy around lean protein. She's like if you stacked six advice guides and three diet books on top of one another, and added a wig.

"This is where you're supposed to cry," Libby says, walking me through the front doors at my new old school, where I come face-to-face with a series of trophies that my brother, Anthony, won. Back when he was only a year or two older and a foot or two taller than I am now.

"Nah," I say, gesturing to a photo of him. "I never cry in front of my brother."

They've Been Talking About Me for Weeks

My chair in homeroom has a weak back leg and every time I breathe in, it squeaks like a fart. (Yay.)

I swear to God it isn't me, but try telling that to the other kids, whose faces and eyes and everythings I can't bring myself to look at, because what if they're making artisanal, handcrafted spitballs to shoot at me? Like the bad ol' days.

I've faced thousands of audience members at a time, but surround me with thirty kids my age and it's like New York didn't even happen to me.

The first bell of the day rings. Allegedly we're supposed to put away our phones and face front for attendance, but almost nobody does. Instead what happens is our homeroom teacher, who is pretty young, comes in and walks directly to my desk, with her arms outstretched toward me like she's a zombie in off-season pastels.

At the very last moment, I think, what the heck, and turn around, but it's *me* she's zombying toward. "We've been talking about you for weeks, Mr. Foster."

Good morning! "Uh, me?"

"Yes, you!" she says, and gestures to the class. I realize that I don't recognize half the faces, that now that I'm in high school, a big portion of the school has been farmed in from other districts and neighborhoods. I thought this was my chance to blend in and save my theatrical tendencies for after school every day. To keep a low profile. But no. Apparently I've been talked about.

"It isn't every day a Broadway star joins homeroom."

"Ha, well," I say, shifting in my seat, making its leg fart (not me!), looking down and expecting snickers from the class. But none come. I look back up. "I mean, I only starred in the show two performances per week, when Jordy—uh, when Jord*an*—would be off for vocal rest. The other shows I was just in the, like . . . like, the chorus."

The homeroom teacher scrunches up her nose like I've insulted her favorite singer or called her dog ugly to its face. "I'm sorry, could I have a show of hands as to how many people *here* have appeared in a Broadway show?" And nobody raises their hand, of course.

I'm sure this sounds as if everything is going enviably well, but something about this on-the-spot show is actually awful, like when somebody tries to describe a funny Tweet hours after reading it. It's never funny when you *talk* about it. Let me be anonymous here. Anonymous means safe.

"Put another way," the teacher says, cracking her knuckles, "*do* raise your hand if you've 'just' been in the chorus on Broadway."

She does air quotes and everything.

I feel something on my elbow, like a small lizard, but it isn't that, it's a boy—a kind of square-looking boy with acne like a zealous pizza, and he says, "Raise your hand, dude," and so I do, half-heartedly.

"You forgot to take attendance and the bell is about to ring again in like forty seconds," says a girl in the back of the room, a kind of kiss-up type who the teacher ignores entirely.

"Okay," she says instead, "who has a question for Mr. Foster? I'll start—what's it like backstage?"

"Did you get paid, like, a lot of money?" a boy asks, and the teacher shoots him a disappointed-cool-older-sister look.

"Do you get nervous before shows?"

"*Fag*," somebody whisper-coughs. Ah, there's the word I was expecting! I *am* home!

"Seriously, though, was it, like, a lot of money, or—?"

"Did you have a curfew—like, could you stay up

all night because your parents weren't there?"

This one stops me. It's all been like a *row-row-row-your-boat* of overlapping questions, as if someone's playing a trick on me and the trick is that *this* school, back home, doesn't think I'm a freak. At least the majority of them don't. They think I'm . . . whatever a not-freak is. I've never had the word for that before.

Not for me, anyway.

But the curfew question, that stops me. "How did you know my parents weren't in New York?" I say, turning around to meet the gaze of a girl with unfortunate neon braces and frizzy hair that could use about three years of hot oil treatments.

"Because you're Nate Foster," she says. "The entire school thinks you're famous. You had your own trending hashtag for a while."

The bell rings twice as hard now, but nobody zips up their bookbags or moves. They just keep looking at me.

Ben Mendoza vs.
Mr. English

It's later, in English class, when the whopper of my first day fully absorbs, like when you leave a clay acne-clearing mask on for too long and it's nearly impossible to wash off.

I'd expected everyone to stare at me like I was and am an alien—they always have—but now it's a different kind of stare. It's like I'm an alien who has come from a more evolved planet. And now I'm here to deliver some kind of message. No pressure?

I suppose that's why I feel uncharacteristically ambitious when our English teacher, Mr. English (can you believe that?), announces we have to come up with a "unique" version of a report on *Great Expectations*, a book by a man named Charlie Dickens.

Unique is sort of what I do, according to rumor.

Several boys fight Mr. English on the assignment.

"Can my unique version of the book report be

that I don't read the book?" asks a boy named Ben Mendoza, who has had to be told to take off his baseball hat twice in ten minutes.

"That would be a no, Mr. Mendoza," Mr. English says. You know those teachers who call kids "Mr." or "Miss?" That's Mr. English.

"Bummer," says Ben.

"Funny, Mr. Mendoza—you're usually among my quieter, more behaved students. Are you showing off for the new boy?"

Big group giggles, here—and Ben Mendoza pulls his ball cap down over his eyes, and I half stab my hand with a pen just to isolate the torture of this moment, this school.

The same girl from homeroom who had a heart attack over our teacher not taking attendance calls out another request here: "Could you give us examples of—" and Mr. English raises his hand as if to say, "Be quiet, child."

I accidentally smile, because for a half moment Mr. English reminds me of New York, where the adults are only condescending because they want to help you. Here it's mostly because they wish they didn't have to be around you. Fact.

Libby's uncle used to work at this school and once told us that teachers get *into* teaching for the right reasons, but at a certain point realize that the majority of children wish they'd disappear under mysterious circumstances, and along with them, the homework would too.

"Listen up, everyone," old, tired Mr. English says. "The rule here is that you have to let me finish and *then* you can ask questions. Because I've been teaching longer than most of your parents have been alive and/or married and/or divorced, and thus can almost always anticipate what your small underdeveloped heads are worrying about." He picks up a coffee mug, doesn't drink, and eyes Ben Mendoza.

Who takes his hat off.

"First," Mr. English says, "I should tell you the SparkNotes version of *Great Expectations*, since most of you will be using that, anyway." This makes me and me alone laugh, but I don't get the scowls I would have gotten in the old days, and in fact, my laughing makes three girls and one neutrally dorky boy laugh too. Look at me, I'm an influencer.

Mr. English fiddles with a Smart Board that proves finicky, and he gives up and is so generally over teaching he doesn't even sigh.

"Off the top of my head: It's the penultimate novel by Charles Dickens, and *penultimate* does not mean *best* or *ultimate*. Does anyone know what it means? Of course you don't. *Penultimate* means *second-to-last*."

Ben shoots his hand up. "Then why not just say

second-to-last. Why does nobody speak English in English class?"

"Because life isn't fair, Mr. Mendoza," Mr. English says. "But thank you for taking your hat off. *That's* the Mr. Mendoza we want."

"When is the assignment due?" cries out a small girl from two rows over.

Okay, *now* Mr. English sighs. Proud of him for mustering the energy. On Broadway, kids and adults are peers—the chorus gets paid the same whether you're eight or eighteen, or eighty—so I'm weirdly pulling for Mr. English, because I know what it's like facing an unruly matinee audience.

"You haven't even let me get to the good part," he says, and, curiously, eyes the American flag in the corner of our room, like it's the only thing in the room that's been through all of these years with him. "There's graveyard encounters in *Great Expectations*, and children stealing alcohol, and—really, it's a whole lot of fun, if you're willing to give Dickens a shot." He pauses, quarter smiles, remembers something good. "Anyway, the assignment is due in a month."

Universal grunts. A month? To read and report on a book, uniquely? You really can't go home again.

"But, listen up, I don't want to read generic reports!" Mr. English says, over the amount of clamor usually reserved for a car accident. "I've done too

69

much reading in my life. Fifty years of terrible book reports on *Great Expectations*. My expectations are, at this point, not even *good*."

He drinks from the mug now, swishes it around a bit, gulps. "There's only so many ways you can summarize Pip—the name of the leading character—learning vital life lessons."

This reminds me that one of the most underrated musicals out there is *Pippin*, which is not as dry as it sounds on paper (chain-link costumes, a love song called "Love Song") because the guy who wrote *Wicked* wrote it, so there's belting.

"I want you to put down your phones for twelve seconds tonight, and make a list of a couple innovative ways you could do an English project about *Great Expectations*. A couple ways that aren't a book report, aren't a summary, and aren't an oral presentation in which you speak in a terrible English accent and I have to pretend to be charmed."

This guy is tough as heck, and half the class is nodding off—but somehow I'm not. I eye the American flag and I swear it waves a little at me, a sign. When the period bell rings, I weirdly know exactly how to get my first-ever B+ in English class. At least, the first-ever B+ that I earn.

That's why I stay behind when the rest of the students take off, swearing under their breath and texting each other. And, in Ben Mendoza's case, putting his baseball hat back on and saying to me, "Welcome to the hardest class in America."

People Who Call Musicals "Plays"

"You wanna do what, now?"

"*E.T.* only rehearsed for five weeks. I can totally pull it off."

Mr. English is either half smiling or half frowning, but whatever it is, it's half.

"Forgive me, Mr. . . . uh—" he says, checking the seating chart for my name, "*Foster*—but, have you considered how time-consuming putting on a full-length play of *Great Expectations* would be?"

People who call musicals "plays" are the trickiest people of all. I clear my throat and breathe into my gut like my New York voice coach taught me to. "Technically, Mr. English, it would be a *musical*."

"Would it, now?" He leans back in his chair. "And who would write the music?"

Huh. "I haven't cracked that part yet."

"And where would you perform the play?"

I step on my own foot in order to localize the pain. "I'd put on the musical in the auditori—" I catch myself. Crap-eroo. We don't have an auditorium anymore. And I sure as heck am not putting this thing on in a lacrosse field.

"Look, if you can find a space to put on your little thing, and you can get enough kids to participate, I suppose it could count as your project—even though it sounds a bit wild to me." He lets the chair spring him back upright, as the bell rings and another group of yawning freshmen enters. "But you're gonna need to figure out a lot of logistics. Last year, a boy named Tansal did *Great Expectations* as a single-page website that he apparently created for free, in about ten minutes. Yours seems a tad overly complicated."

"Thank you."

"Don't thank me yet," Mr. English says, handing me a late slip for my next class. "I'm a tough grader."

But I wave the slip around like I'm Charlie going to the chocolate factory, and head out.

"Oh, and Mr. Foster," Mr. English says when I'm at his door. "Who exactly is going to direct this thing?"

I lean against the wall and say, "I am, Mr. English," with a kind of wise-guy smile. Except I accidentally lean against a switch that turns off the classroom lights.

Everyone Loves a Montage!

The next part, if it were a movie, would be called a montage, which I think is French for: "All the good parts, set to a great song." So, picture your favorite song, and a whole sequence where I run around asking for favors.

Right at lunch, I text Libby, and we meet up outside the shop class. I point inside, feeling harried. "What's up with the fact that the shop class has no machinery now?"

Libby looks at me like I've transformed into a regular boy. "You mean like buzz saws and stuff?"

"And stuff, yes."

"Yeah, the school board eliminated all that. Said that manufacturing jobs are on their way out. Now they just teach us how to build our own apps in there."

I glance back in, panicked to see a bunch of students quietly working over iPads. "Well, how am I going to build a set if I don't have an army of cheap labor?!"

Libby picks something off her shirt. "What are you even talking about?"

"I'm putting on a musical version of *Great Expectations* for my English project. It's due in like a month. I'm thinking first-B-plus-*ever* territory here."

Now she perks up. "Do you need a casting director?"

"Hilarious, I thought you'd say 'female lead.'"

She waves her hands around. "Nah, overrated. The joy is behind the scenes, where you can boss people around."

The teacher in the not-shop class comes outside and says, "Can I help you two?" in an unhelpful way.

"Only if you have the ability to create a complex Dickensian London backdrop using apps," I want to say, but instead shake my head like I speak a different language. Which, I do.

The language of Broadway, duh.

Libby grabs my bookbag by the fabric hook and pulls me away.

"Yes indeed," she says as a strange segue. "By my calculations, we'll need to start casting right away . . ." And I stop her.

"Libster, *I'm* directing. And adapting. And having to, like, figure out the music part of the musical. So maybe before we cast the show, we figure out what the show *is*."

"Ah," she says, "like if it's a *Hamilton* scale or it's a *Scottsboro Boys* scale."

And I say, "Def," and Libby's eyes squint up like she's thinking of something.

"What?" I say, and she goes, "I'm late to lunch and just remembered it's turkey salad day."

Yeck. "What is *that*?"

"The school's health initiative program—but don't worry, because I see you worrying: They have this blue cheese dressing that is like seventy percent hydrogenated, so it's delicious and you can dip things in it that you bring from home."

She pulls out half a baguette from her bookbag, and I love her.

I follow Lib toward the cafeteria, stepping over spilled pencils and a bunch of unfinished homework and one lone, half-chewed-up eraser.

"What you'll need, more than anything else," Libby says, now in full-on producer mode, "is a space to put on the musical."

See, at least she calls it a musical. She gets it. This is why you keep a best friend by your side. Or, in our case, two feet in front of me, owning the hallways and now the cafeteria.

"Any ideas?" I say, right as we're bypassing the

fruit stand and heading straight for the carb station.

"Only one," Libby goes, grabbing a side of pudding. "When is P.E. for you?"

I shudder. "Why bring up something so terrible when we're talking about something so beautiful?"

She slides the pudding back and grabs some kind of approximation of a "health cobbler," which apparently has 14 grams of "vital nutrients," according to a small handwritten sign.

"You're not thinking big enough," Libby says. "The gym's got wooden floors, a lot of lighting, a decent sound system, and in-the-round seating with the bleachers. Put on your show there."

This is all happening so fast. It's such a good idea I almost chug an unpaid-for chocolate milk to celebrate. "You're brilliant."

"Duh," she says. "But good luck getting past the coach."

Right. Crap-eroo. The man who helped Anthony bring home about twenty different trophies in six different disciplines. I'm basically back to square one. Picture your favorite song ending. The montage is over.

"Natey," Libby says, gesturing toward my out-of-date jeans. "You just spilled chocolate milk all over yourself."

President of the Dork Union

So I'm already sweating, because the gym smells like one hundred years of foot-ozone.

Mind you, I'm not sweating because I'm actually, like, moving, or anything outlandish like that. Other than my foot tapping, outside the coach's office, between classes.

He's on the phone, hollering at somebody about helmets, when my pocket vibrates. And now I'm seven times as sweaty, because just when I'd stopped obsessing over him, it's Jordan. On the set of his TV show. Sending me the cutest selfie in the history of selfies.

I'm not sure how to reply. His eyes are way too blue and his skin is so, like, pure, that there's no way he's not in a thousand pounds of makeup.

"you look like a drag queen, in a great way" I start to reply, but autocorrect turns it into "yow! Looks like a drag" because apparently my phone is a cowboy?

Regardless, time stands still and a hundred other clichés that are clichés for a reason, when I hear, "Why are you in my gym?"

Oh, right. "Coach," I say like a four-year-old, just namin' nouns.

"That's my name. What's the problem?"

The problem is, I haven't responded to Jordan's text, which makes me hate the gym more than I usually do, which is truly saying something.

"I have a favor to ask."

"Right," the coach says. "I assume you're trying to get out of class because of a bogus condition like asthma. You'll have to go to the nurse and get her to write a note."

There is an outside chance that I'm biting off more than I should be chewing on my first day ever of regular-kid high school. Only time will tell. Watch this space.

Coach turns on himself and whaps the doorframe with his shoulder and grunts like a Neanderthal. But he's got me all wrong.

"No, actually—I'm here to ask if I can use the gym. For, like, a thing."

His neck goes the color of purple that I experimented with back in New York, when Heidi was on a date and I found some of her blush. But makeup isn't really for me and I have to say this color purple is not really for Coach, either.

"*Use* my gym?" he says, or grunts, really.

He is basically the second-to-last guy on the evolution chart, hunched over, not yet ready for a suit and tie but still capable of making your life horrible.

"Yeah, like, to put on a musical show-thing—for credit! For English credit."

He turns fully back around to me, and attempts to crack his knuckles but can't, because his hands are too meaty. God, I hope my hands are never that meaty. How would I open a jar of peanut butter at midnight for my second dinner, with hands so meaty?

"You're Anthony Foster's little brother, aren't you," he says, squinting like there's a surprise wind in here.

"The one and only," I attempt, but my voice cracks and it comes out like an apology.

"And you wanna do what, now? Some kind of Broadway thingy here?"

To his credit, he seems to think I'm crazy, but he's not, like, disgusted with me. Just looking at me like I'm a butterfly who's loose in his gorilla cage. Could be worse.

"I mean, technically, not Broadway, because not New York"—I hold for laughter. Not coming. Not coming. "But, uh, yeah—I have to do a *Great Expectations* project and I want to put on an all-singing, all-dancing version. And—" I gesture to the space like it's a million-dollar listing on one of those home TV shows Aunt Heidi pretends not to be obsessed with. "Look at this place. It's sort of . . . ideal for an audience?"

He snorts, hocks a loogie, spits it into a trash can. He's still squinting.

"Fine."

He turns and whaps his shoulder into the side of the doorframe again, and I realize maybe he's doing it on purpose. Like when you are at the zoo, and a rhino rubs its back against a tree.

"Fine, as in: yes?" I say.

"You can *have* the *gym*."

My head jerks back so hard and with such surprise force that I finally crack a tricky neck vertebrae that's been fused stuck for two months, ever since I had to wear a ten-pound fiberglass alien head costume back in *E.T.*

"Um, thank you, Coach!"

"Provided," he says, holding up one meaty finger that's the size of two regular fingers, "you cast my niece."

He holds up his phone now, to show me a picture of her—and I recognize her. It's the frizzy-haired girl from my homeroom, the girl so dorky even *I* thought, *Wow, what a dork.* And for a while *I* was considered the king of dorks here. Like, if dorks had a union, I'd be the president.

"She's excited that a fellow theater kid is ten feet away from her in homeroom. She's been talking about it for a week. She's different, a loner. If you want to use the gym, you have to cast my niece."

I snap my fingers. "Done," I say.

Aunt Heidi always says the showbiz is all about connections, "who you know." So, sure, if I have to cast the coach's niece in the chorus in order to use this expansive space—suddenly the gym seems magical—then, of course. Duh.

"Give her one of the leads," the coach says, kicking the door shut on me.

The ozone-sneaker smell comes back to me in a wave, and my phone vibrates, and Jordan has responded: "uh, it's not a 'drag'? It's literally almost a lead in a TV show?"

Apparently I *did* send that autocorrected text by accident. Yow.

And as I'm typing back my reply about "sorry" and "autocorrect" and "nvm, start over: you look amazing," the coach opens the door and says, "Get to your next class, Anthony's little brother."

Bad British Accents

"Start over," Libby says, "and talk slower. You're making me seasick."

I'm pacing in her basement.

Libby's mom has left us celery with low-fat peanut butter and we thanked her and then immediately ordered pizza on Libby's Domino's app, because she has the kind of mom who lets you store her credit card number on your phone.

"It's just, now I'm nervous, because *Great Expectations* is basically a cast of thousands." I've got my phone out and I'm looking at the character list on the internet and reading it to Libby. "How am I going to find this many talented students in *one* high school in Pennsylvania?"

Libby holds up her hand. "Couple things. First: don't be ignorant."

"I'm not!"

"You're being a smiiiidge ignorant."

Oh, in Western PA we say "ignorant" for "arrogant." Not kidding. If I say "arrogant," though, it doesn't mean ignorant. For *actual*-ignorant, we say "uneducated."

Another reason I should have stayed in New York.

"So, yeah," Libby says, "let's get the ignorance under wraps."

I reach for a celery stick because at least if I'm being insulted it can be padded by food.

"Second," she says, "you've been speaking in an *incredibly* vague British accent ever since coming back from New York, and I need to know literally right now if you're aware of this."

I choke on the celery. "I am n—" Like, I'm choking. I am deceased. Okay, maybe I'm just laughing. "You are ridiculous. I am so not speaking in anything but my regular, nasal voice." She fiddles with her phone, holds it up—and then plays back my voice, because apparently she's been recording me. Sneaky.

But—"Wow, *yeah*." I'm speaking in the weirdest faux-Cockney accent. She's right.

"Like, I know you've been to Broadway now," Libby says, quickly sending off a selfie to a sophomore on the soccer team, "but I'm going to need you to take the attitude *and* the accent from a nine, where you are now, to, at most, a three."

I swallow the celery. "Got it."

"Back to our show."

It's hot down here, stuffy, and she oozes off the sofa and onto the shag rug and puts her feet up on a cushion. "I think you just build the show around the cast who shows up to audition."

"Wait—but what if *nobody* shows up? To audition?!"

"Right, so. Again, I'm sort of the unofficial president of the Nate Foster fan club—don't let it go to your head—so I feel confident I can rally the dorks to show up for you. High school is better than middle school, trust your girl. When they tore the roof off the auditorium last month, I got five altos to picket with me. So I *know* they've got friends, and I know *those* friends know some tenors. We'll be fine."

"Ugh, if you say so. I guess." It's just that if I can't pull off *Great Expectations* as a musical, then I don't have something to obsess over that isn't Jordan or New York. Like, I've already chosen *Great Expectations* as my unofficial freshman major.

Libby grins like a billboard that's made of teeth. "It's fun, ya know?"

"What is?"

"Seeing you nervous again. I was worried you'd come back a hundred percent cocky."

"You just said I'm a *nine* on the ignorant scale."

Libby throws her hands around like a flock of

85

lost birds. "I'm exaggerating. You're still the same old Natey. For instance, the way you keep checking your phone to see if you-know-who is gonna text you tonight."

Face: melting. Hope it at least takes off a few zits. "I'm actually so over Jordan," I say, choking on words and not celery now. "For the record. In case you're secretly audio-recording this, too."

"Surrre," she says. She's on her feet now, marching to a crafts closet where her mom keeps supplies. Can you imagine something so fun? Like, an entire Michael's, but in your basement?

"What are you doing?" I say.

"Getting out poster board. We're making signs to plaster all over the school, so people know to show up for auditions this weekend."

"Do we need permission?"

"Of course, but it's better to ask for forgiveness later than deal with the front office first."

I mean, I'm telling you, she has a plan for everything, this girl.

She gets out stencils, glitter, a bunch of star stickers, spreads them out on a coffee table. She's beaming. But it all looks . . . troublingly jazzy.

"If I may?" I say, and she looks up at me like I'm interrupting a Bar Mitzvah. "I mean, it's a show set in old-timey days, in England. I feel like *maybe* we want to use browns, and various neutral shades. If we're designing a logo. Instead of, like, glitter. Right now." She uncaps a marker. "Again, just an observation."

A quick refresher on *Great Expectations* is in order, right? Lord knows I don't expect you to actually read it yourself. That's what I'm here for.

So, it stars and is narrated by a boy named Pip (imagine being named Pip—literally the other boys would be making fun of you *as* you're leaving the hospital on the day of your birth). Pip is British, so probably has slightly questionable teeth but a fantastic haircut, and when he's young, he falls *hard* for a wealthy chick named Estella, who is the adopted daughter of a crazy old cat lady named Miss Havisham—which would be a great role for Broadway legend Christine Ebersole, if I were staging this on Broadway, which I should be. The entire book—I know this, because in the forty-eight hours since Mr. English assigned the project, I've read the SparkNotes (twice!!)—is about Pip being literally *obsessed* with Estella, even though she ghosts him constantly and is, like, *boy, bye*, all the time. And at one point, Pip becomes a blacksmith, I think I read. Or a locksmith, but I don't think it matters. He's a something-smith, and he's basically super-into a girl who doesn't want him back. The book opens in a graveyard scene that involves a convict jumping out to scare Pip, and it will stun and frighten my future audience in the gym, once we cast this show and begin rehearsals. And get me on my way toward my first-ever B+.

Assuming Libby can actually "rally the dorks" to audition.

So, yeah: I'm just not sure if a glittery logo, which Libby is mid-design on right now, is going to serve the story of an obsessive English boy named Pip.

"*We* aren't designing a logo," Libby says, fanning the poster board to make the glue dry. "We're making audition posters. Very different intention."

I slump into the seat that was Libby's rabbit's favorite chair, when Libby had a rabbit. Cutest little guy. The rabbit's name was Marin Mazzie, an amazing Broadway soprano with a very healthy chest voice.

"Like, different, *how*?" I say.

"Auditions are all about getting attention, being flashy—throwing as wide a net as possible out to sea, and seeing what you catch. For instance, you getting cast in *E.T.*"

"Thank you." I think.

"The show poster itself is totally different. The show poster is about selling to an audience you hope buys the ticket. Don't ask me how I know these things, it's a gift and a curse."

She tests out a pink marker and my veins aren't wide enough to accommodate the onslaught of rush-hour blood. Pink just feels *so wrong* for *Great Expectations*—but we agreed, yesterday at lunch, that we wouldn't butt into each other's departments.

Oh, that would be good for you to know, ha!

Here's the title page for our Playbill program that Libby typed up for my approval, during physical chemistry class this morning:

NATE FOSTER (director)
&
LIBBY JACKSON
(designer, producer, casting director)

Present

Charles Dickens's
"Great Expectations:
a shocking new musical"

in the gym on November 19, at night,
before Thanksgiving break
$5 tickets and also ~cash bar in lobby~

Libby, who knows a ton more than I do about the history of advertising (her mom let her stream *Mad Men*) explained to me how billing works. Since my name is *first* (the prime position), it's smaller than *her* name, which comes second (only fair).

The title itself is pretty famous—ask any nearby

parent, one of them is 70 percent certain to have heard of *Great Expectations*—so we don't have to make a big deal out of it. Hence, why it's the same font size as the rest.

And why our names are so big.

"Do we really want to say 'cash bar,'" I said to her when she sent me the title page, earlier today. And she said, "We aren't making money on tickets, we're making money on *drinks*," and pointed to a statistic that Red Bull and Mountain Dew account for almost all of the daily water most high schoolers get. I can't remember where she heard that statistic, but it sounds exactly right to me.

"Ta-da!" She holds up the audition poster and, honestly, it looks fantastic. Violently sparkly. Here it is:

ARE YOU TALENTED?
ARE YOU SUuuUuuuUuUuRE?
Come to Libby Jackson's backyard
THIS Sunday afternoon at 11 a.m.
for a ****rare opportunity***
British accents a plus!!

"I can't believe you did all of that by hand."

You know how there's always one kid in your class who can do expert hand-drawn bubble letters? That's our girl Libby.

"You're a great producer," I say.

"Slash designer, slash casting director."

"Duh."

She waves the poster back and forth to dry all the ink and glue. And glitter. And a few odd googly-eyes, left over from the long-ago summer when we put on *Phantom* with sock puppets.

"And you, my dear," she says, affecting a truly terrible British accent, the kind that routinely earns older women Emmy nominations, "are destined to be a great little director."

By the way, I've been home for basically a *week*, for those keeping track. Everything in New York happens, statistically, a hundred times faster than anywhere else. I've brought that energy back home, like I'm an explorer returning with faraway spices.

Libby and I fist-bump, but are terrible at it and it hurts my wrist a little. I miss when we used to hug, but now that I kiss boys and she has boobs, it doesn't feel as normal.

"Director, yes—*and* lead actor, in addition to director, possibly, if you cast me!" I almost say, but it's not my place. We haven't had auditions yet, so we don't know where it will all end up. She's the casting director. If she doesn't see me as Pip (the lead), she doesn't see me as Pip (the part I'm best for). Art isn't "about" suffering, but it's also not about suffering, if that makes sense?

"Libby?!" we hear from the top of the stairs, and see her bug-eyed mom looking her version of mad, which is sort of bemused. Note to moms: Be the kind of mom who gets bemused more often than mad. "It's nine-thirty p.m.! Did one of you order a pizza?!"

A Short but Important Note on School Policies

One good thing about having a dad who likes to disappear from his family into a toolshed for hours at a time is that he most definitely has at least one roll of duct tape for you to "borrow" without his explicit knowledge.

In my dad's case, he has *five* rolls, just sitting around, half-used, next to his screwdrivers and fishing kit. Don't ask me why.

One of these duct tape rolls comes in mighty handy when, the next day, I'm attempting to plaster Libby's handmade posters all over the hallways on the second floor of school, to alert the masses to the weekend auditions for my show.

I get caught in the act. "What's this all about, new boy?" says Ben Mendoza, the kid in the baseball cap who likes to give Mr. English a tough time—but who,

I've come to learn after a handful of classes, is also his secret star student.

Every boy is basically a secret in a ball cap.

"Auditions for my musical version of *Great Expectations*," I say. And I'm sort of proud of it, and sort of proud of *that*. Maybe high school Nate just *owns* his full Nateness. "It's for our English project. Otherwise, I wouldn't be doing it. Obviously. Like, there are better things to musicalize, trust me."

"Oh, nice," Ben says. I wait for him to make fun of me, but he doesn't. He says *nice* and it's just that. Nice.

"You should come!" I say. "Auditions are at my friend Libby's house."

Ben points to the poster, only half taped to the wall. "Yeah, I see that. Hard to miss. It's all very glittery."

"Her idea!" I say, or shout. "I'm the director, but Libby's the designer. Among, like, a million other jobs."

"I don't think you want me in your cast," Ben says. "According to my mom, I have zero natural talent!"

He grunt-laughs, and backs away from me—again, goodbyes are always hard to predict in Jankburg—but I tear off a piece of duct tape with my teeth and say, "Gee, your mom sounds super sweet," and Ben Mendoza says, "Yeah, she's super not!"

I smack a piece of tape down on a corner of the poster. "You should come, seriously," I say. "I'm going to need boys, and your mom could be wrong. You could have *more* than zero talent."

He full-on laughs now, but doesn't commit to showing up for the tryout. He just goes, "Later, Foster." And I say, "Later, Mendoza"—and it's the first time I've ever called a boy by his last name, and now I see why Anthony always did that, with *his* friends. It's sort of fun, like an instant nickname you don't have to try too hard at.

Three posters later, when I'm nearly out of duct tape, the principal herself chases me down a back hallway, and tells me I need "a permit" (literally, a permit) for such an apparently flagrant violation of school policies.

I try to affect the *Aw, gee,* and *Who, me?* innocent-kid thing I used to do when I was little.

I mean, I'm still little—definitely on the short side of the boys in high school—but my voice is low enough now that when I bat my eyelashes, I probably look like I'm making *fun* of someone adorable instead of being someone adorable.

"Maybe 'permit' is too strong a word," the principal says, crossing her arms at me. "But you definitely need permission. These walls are very old and duct tape could damage them."

I'm telling you, adults worry about the dumbest things.

So I go back and tear them all down, and then: "operation audition announcement didn't go so hot," I text Libby, with a ☹ or seven thrown in, and chase it with: "did you know u need a PERMIT to put up posters in this joint?"

"of course i knew that, but being risky is what makes life in Pennsylvania worth living."

We make a date to meet over "health cobbler" at lunch. Turns out I'm not fully committed to my brand-new, all-lean-protein diet. Maybe next week.

"Worry not, little diva," Libby says, when she spies me not licking the plate, a rarity for me. "We're not the only theater kids anymore. It's *high school*. The dorks will arrive." She grabs my plate and finishes my cobbler. "You even whisper the word *audition*, and the dorks always arrive."

Like She's Thirty, or Something

If we are lucky, I'm thinking as I bike over to Libby's on the morning of the audition, we'll get nine kids to show up, tops. Nine would be okay. A nice number.

With me, as Pip, the lead, rounding out the cast at ten.

But when I'm four blocks away, heading into Libby's neighborhood—whose fences are wooden instead of my family's chain-link—I see a whole group of kids gathered. Actually, lined up, snaking around the block.

"Crap-eroo."

And I wonder if we counter-programmed the auditions for the day of some popular kid's birthday party.

But then I get a text: "you literally won't believe how many people I recruited last night over like 40 separate group-texts to come to the audition. I said we'd provide chips and dip for anyone who showed up. KIDS LOVE FREE CHIPS AND DIP!! Also, we need ice for sodas. Please pick up ice. Just that!!!!"

But I can't. There are no convenience stores near Libby's house; it's that kind of subdivision that doesn't have advertising. It's just two-storey houses with all their windows intact.

Anyway, I burst through her front door after plowing through a pretty big crowd on her front yard. Her mom is out there directing traffic, getting people lined up, making sure the boys' shirts are tucked in to audition, as if she's getting them ready for school photo day.

"I mean," I say.

"I meannn," Libby says.

"I mean!" I say again, and she and I fist-bump again and it hurts (again), and she hands me a Diet Coke in a cup that honestly does need ice.

"Aren't musicals the best?" I say, and accidentally burp on "best," and Libby goes, "My lady," and we giggle and decide to start the casting process right away. Saturdays are our nights for YouTubing vintage cabaret shows, you see, and it's already almost noon.

• • •

"I thought I would just sort of read from the book?" says the first boy, and Libby goes, "Great, that's exactly what we were going to ask you to do."

Then she pulls out her phone and writes, for me to

see, "*That's a good idea, right, for people just to read from the book?*" and I nod yes. Great idea.

That's exactly how we'll do the script, I decide, right here, because directors have to be decisive. Just highlight the lines Dickens wrote, as dialogue, and use all the other descriptions as stage directions.

It's all coming together.

And as the first auditioner starts reading one of the hundred boring parts of *Great Expectations*, Libby texts her mom, "Tell every person in line to pick a part from the book to read, and we WILL NOT HESI-TATE to cut them off if they don't demonstrate emotional complexity. Thx!☺"

And her mom texts back, "Calm down, Sofia Coppola," which is a movie reference that I don't "get" until Libby explains it to me, moments after the boy stops reading and Libby and I both dismiss him without consulting each other, because he doesn't have the range for our vision of the show.

Cute shoes, though.

"You're going to kill me," I say, and she goes, "Did you fart?" and I go, "No!" like I'm truly offended (I am), and then say: "I just feel like . . . so many people are giving up a Saturday afternoon to be here, and—"

"No."

She looks at her clipboard and yells, "Next!" at her mom on the stairs.

And I go, "Wait, how did you know what I was going to say?"

"Because you're Nate, Nate. And just because someone auditions does not mean we have to give them a part."

"But, what about even the chorus?"

"What about it. You said you wanted sopranos that make you laugh and belters that make you weep, basically a cast full of all-stars. You were very specific. I took notes." She holds up literal notes. "I'm your casting director and I'm trying to bring your vision to life."

"Am I . . . interrupting?" we hear, but don't look up from the table, which we've set up in Libby's basement next to her former bunny's favorite lounge chair. "Like, should I come back?"

"Give us twelve seconds, dear," Libby says, like she's thirty or something.

"I totally hear you right now, Lib," I say, a technique I picked up from Heidi. People just want to be heard. *Then* you can ignore them. "I just think: We might want to remain open to really leading with kindness here, and letting anyone who wants to be a part of the arts be a part of the arts. Their auditorium got torn down, ya know?"

Libby scowls at me like I'm a math problem. "You've changed—you're, like, nicer and more grown-up now—and I don't hate it, and I hate that I don't hate it."

She pops an orange wedge into her mouth (her mom already took the peel off, she's seriously the greatest lady), looks up, and whispers, "Oof, the hair on this one. It's like we don't even need a wig budget."

"Hi!" I say, too loudly, because now I see that it's the coach's niece who's standing before us. Yikes. I still haven't told Libby we are required to cast her if we want the gym. Which we do! The acoustics alone really have to be heard to be believed.

"I'm very happy to be here," the girl says, and my heart breaks for her, because nothing to me is more risky or beautiful than someone choosing not to be snarky.

"Thanks, kiddo," Libby says. "What have you prepared for us?"

"I thought I'd take a stab at Miss Havisham," the girl says, naming the part you'd put Meryl Streep in if you wanted awards recognition. She's the crazed old cat lady with the adoptive daughter. She's meaty. She's the lead. She's basically exactly what I promised the coach I'd give his niece, who stands before us now with the approximate innocence of a toddler in the middle of rush-hour traffic.

And I bellow, "Terrific!" right as Libby says, "The central female role, eh?"

And because Libby's sentence is longer, she wins, and I want to push my chair away from the table and into a hole.

"I mean, I thought I'd try?" says the girl, and I catch her name on the sign-in sheet—Paige, an old-fashioned name for a girl reading an old part.

"Go for it, Paige," I say, and Libby shoots me an *Are you running this audition or am I?* look. And Paige, God love her, goes: "*Please*: Call me Miss Havisham," and winks.

I giggle, but Libby snorts.

Paige closes her eyes and shakes her head back and forth a couple times like she's going to wrestle an animal for money. And then she opens her copy of *Great Expectations* to the middle, and I can see she's highlighted a part to read, and it really moves me. I know what it feels like to not have the chance at something, before you even speak.

"*So proud, so proud, moaned Miss Havisham, pushing away her grey hair with both her hands,*" Paige says, and she's moaning, and she's pushing her hair away, and Libby holds up her hand like they do on televised talent competitions to signal they've had enough. "Just great," Libby says, "great."

And Paige goes, "G-great?" Because in six seconds, greatness is hard to tell, unless you're listening to the *Newsies* album.

"Are you willing to dye your hair grey?" Libby says, but not in a mean way. "For the show?"

"I mean . . . wow? I guess?"

Libby pops gum and waits it out.

"I mean . . . *sure!*"

"*There* we go," Libby says, and Paige giggles like you do when you want to die, and pushes her definitely-not-grey hair behind her ears. She's the kind of kid whose ears still aren't pierced. She's pure as heck.

"If you're willing to go grey, the part is yours."

I can barely believe it. This is . . . so easy. Toooo easy?

"Thank you, for real!" Paige yells, and approaches the desk to hug us.

I leap up to hug her back (duh), but Libby remains planted in her chair, and simply shakes Paige's hand like they're a pair of female senators who are only nice to each other to further the women's movement.

When Paige leaves, Libby yells, "Mom, will you tell the next kid to hold on just a second!" and her mom goes, "Sure!" from the top of the stairs.

I'm about to blurt out, "Paige is really solid, right? Like a total natural!" when Libby goes, "That oughtta make *the coach* happy, right?"

And if Libby had right then turned into forty baby eels, I'd probably be less surprised.

"You *did* promise the role to the coach, no?"

"How did you—"

"I know everything, Nate. While you were busy learning the ins and outs of Broadway, I was nailing my freshman psych class. I've got a B-plus in mental gymnastics. Practically an A, if you round up."

She taps her head, twice, and says: "From now on, we share all decisions about the show, up front. Especially the sneaky ones. You're semi-famous now. Everything you do spreads through the school like fire. Or lice. Or lice on fire."

I realize I'm sitting on my hand and that it's gone tingly. So I shake it out, and nod my head too.

"Deal?"

"Deal."

And this time when we fist-bump, it's just right.

"Okay, Ma!" Libby yells, dumping the plate of oranges into a garbage can and pulling out a Snickers. "Send in the next kid."

Poor Connection Quality

One thing I learned today is that if you're going to write your upcoming-first-day-of-rehearsal speech on your phone, you should hold it under your desk instead of out in the open.

"Mr. Foster, I appreciate your enthusiasm for the project." This is Mr. English, pulling me aside after class. Yet again. "But it won't do you much good to get an A on your play but flunk the rest of English class. That's still failing."

"It's a musical," I want to say, but instead I channel my best actor self and pretend like what he just said is a beautiful piece of poetry. "Mr. English," I say, nodding my head a bunch, "that makes a whole lot of sense."

"So we're good?" he says, and I say, "We're good, *but*—" and he sighs and turns back around and drops a stack of papers on the corner of his desk. A paper I sort of forgot was due today, hence my being kept after class.

"But?"

"But this project is a big deal to me." I hold up my phone. "This speech? That I've written, to say to my cast at the first rehearsal this coming weekend? I'm pouring my whole heart into it, and honestly, I wouldn't be writing it if it weren't for your English class, and—"

"Very moving, Mr. Foster," he says, retrieving the stack of papers and fanning them absentmindedly. He's got the look on his face of a grown-up when they're thinking of a tropical destination where no children are allowed. "But unfortunately, I'm not able to grade a speech that's stuck on your phone. So, unless that's a speech about how adverbs ruin otherwise good pieces of writing, a paper that was due twenty-five minutes ago, leave it out of my class."

He pulls out his own phone, sits down, and begins typing.

"What are—are you texting someone right now?" I say, shocked. Appalled! We're having a conversation.

"Yes," he says, throwing his feet up on his desk. "It's *after* class. This is the *appropriate* time to be playing on your phone." And he waves me off.

• • •

There's a big ancient bathroom stall on the third floor of the school, behind a strange failure of a planetarium (halfway through construction in the mid-nineties, the school board ran out of money, so they turned it into a teachers' napping room). Anyway, no kid ever comes to this stall because who wants to do three sets of stairs if you don't have to, but I'm hiding in here during a free period, and going over my first-day-of-rehearsal speech, and it dawns on me that a good audience to try it out on is Jordan.

Also, I miss his face.

My FaceTime call doesn't go through, it just rings and rings, when Jordan texts me: "Gimme 2, I'm going back to my trailer."

And, like, great, right? Jordan is calling me from a TV-set trailer and I'm in a bathroom stall. The glamour of a long-distance relationship!

My side rings. I let it go two times, enough not to seem overly excited.

"Jordy!" I say, "surprised" to be hearing from him.

He flops down on a tiny couch in his big trailer, and goes, "Are you ready?" and I think, "For what?" but don't say it, because I want him to always think that *yes, I'm ready,* for anything.

He angles his phone to a gigantic bleeding gash in his forehead.

I'm screaming.

"It's just makeup!" he says, but I'm still screaming. The bathroom stall turns into a haunted house, echoing my own shout off the walls and back at me in horror-movie surround sound.

"It's so realistic!"

"Well, if it isn't clear, I die in this episode," Jordan says, super casual, now chewing on ice. If he ruins those perfect teeth, his mother *and* I will kill him.

On the metal maroon bathroom stall wall, I see a scratched piece of graffiti—*Mr. English sucks*—that looks like it's a hundred years old; like he's been teaching here for centuries, and that maybe this bathroom really is old enough to be haunted. I reach out and run my finger over the graffiti, and it's so rusted out and sharp that it almost hurts.

"But don't worry," I hear, and look back, and Jordan has set his phone down against the dressing mirror to futz with a little curl on the end of his hair. I love that curl. "They bring me back in two episodes and apparently I have a monologue as a ghost that my manager predicts could get Emmys buzz."

"Oh!" I say, trying my best not to eye-roll/snort. "That's why I was calling. I'm practicing a speech. Not as a ghost, ha-ha. As, ya know, me."

Jordan's eyes flick over and I hear an adult come into his conversation, and then he says to me, "Make it quick, I'm back on set in two minutes."

He pauses for a sec, and tilts his head, and goes, "Hey, I miss you, by the way."

He misses me.

Hey.

He misses me.

By the way.

Hey, he misses me, by the way. A boy with a curl like that misses me.

I want to pull out a penny and scratch *Jordan doesn't suck* in graffiti in this stall, or on my bicep, if I had a bicep. I suddenly see the appeal of having a tattoo—he said he misses me. I'd love that in permanent ink.

"Gee, don't say you miss me back or anything!" he goes, taking a swig of soda. And I go, "No, I totally do! It's just, I'm, like, distracted. This is my only free period and I'm just waiting for a teacher to barge in on me."

Jordan gets up and smoothes back his eyebrows in the mirror. "So," he says, "are you gonna do your first-day-of-whatever speech for me?"

"You have to run," I say, brushing it off, "so maybe later." I don't want to ruin the mood or the moment or the missing-me.

"Nate," he goes, pulling on an uncharacteristically Jordan hoodie. Must be a costume for his death scene. "Just gimme the gist."

"The gist?" I look up, to try and see the speech in my head. "The gist is: Welcome to the first day of rehearsal. Prepare to work really hard. And if you're lucky, maybe you'll meet a great friend here . . . or something even more."

I'm trying so hard to send little Nate-waves of flirtation energy through the screen—but I'm getting this annoying Poor Connection Quality message on my phone. All I can hear is, "Nate? I can't hear you, if you're talking. Natey?"

I'm yelling *Yes!* back, but he's not hearing me.

"I gotta run!"

Poor Connection Quality. Poor Connection Quality.

Poor Connection Quality.

One, Two, Three—Improv!

On Broadway, we have "bagel meet and greets." It's for the first day of rehearsal, when the producer supplies carb platters, and everyone stands around drinking orange juice or coffee (which I've heard is growth-stunting), and pretending not to be nervous, and "accidentally" spouting out their extensive résumés to each other.

Libby and I decided we'd do donuts and water for our first rehearsal. We're also announcing who got cast in what part—so vast, unchecked amounts of sugar should help offset any heartbreak. That's the theory, anyway.

The kids arrive to Libby's basement in small groups, some carpooling, some riding over and leaving their bikes on Libby's front lawn. It's that kind of neighborhood. No one's gonna steal your bike.

You'd think people would be super loud at a first

rehearsal, talking a mile a minute as they make the loop down Libby's spiral staircase. But nah. It's pretty silent.

Then Libby's mom brings out the donuts and it's like a Christmas party, it gets so hyper.

Everyone's going to town when I realize we're already six minutes after the hour—that's no way to run a rehearsal!—so Libby clears her voice, steps up onto a chair, and says: "Look at our amazing cast! Just look at you!"

In New York, people would burst into applause, at this point, but here they just murmur-laugh.

She double-bops her eyebrows at me and says, "I believe our director has a little something he'd like to say, to kick us off into our journey." I'm proud of her, because I taught her that on Broadway, when words fail you, you just mention your "journey" and people nod.

"Um!" I say, like an idiot. My knee starts to vibrate and I can picture it burrowing a hole into her carpet, so I lift my leg and shake it out, like I'm some kind of athlete. And before I can launch into my welcome speech, Libby has rerouted this journey, and is giving a speech of her own.

"As your producer," she says, now stepping off the chair and onto her old pine coffee table, "it's my job to make sure there's no big bumps on the way to opening night."

A semi-random girl yells, "I already know I have to miss next weekend's rehearsal because of my cousin's Bar Mitzvah!" and this creates a small uproar that is difficult to tone down.

That's when I notice Ben Mendoza—the homeroom boy in the hat, with "zero talent" according to Mrs. Mendoza—slink in, from Libby's kitchen upstairs, the last to arrive.

Which isn't so weird. There's always somebody late to rehearsal. Always.

The weird part is: We didn't cast Ben. As in: He didn't show up to audition last week.

"People," Libby says, clapping, "people."

I'm three bites into what I call a "thinking donut"— the kind that's dusted with so much sugar, it actually jump-starts the best areas of your brain—when Libby says, "So, *Nate*, like I said, is there *anything* you'd like to say to your loud, beautiful cast?"

From the crowd comes the heckling of a six-foot-tall freshman boy who, back in middle school, would have called me a mean name here. Instead, he appears to have butterflied himself into an artist, while I was away—high school really *is* different—and he goes: "C'mon, Broadway boy!" in a purposefully goofy voice that makes two of the girls who I've heard haven't had their first kiss yet laugh too hard.

"Thanks, Libby." I wave at her, up there on the

coffee table with her hands on her hips. "I'm gonna stay down here where it's safe."

Nobody laughs.

Somebody's phone goes off and somebody else coughs, and I pull open my iPhone speech to read. But in my sweaty haste, my big dumb thumb highlights the entire paragraph and deletes the thing in three seconds flat.

One, two, three—improv!

"So, here's the thing, as your director," I say, punting. I slowly turn like I'm the world's most theatrical chicken rotisserie. There is nothing quite like eighteen kids staring at you expectantly to make you need to pee and puke at the same time. On Broadway, I wouldn't bat my eyes at two thousand strangers staring me down. Here it's different. You don't have an orchestra pit between you, as a buffer.

"I know better than maybe anyone what it's like to not always get the part you want. And I know how weird it is to put on makeup and to, like, try to balance schoolwork with rehearsals."

"Just skip the schoolwork!" some kid yells, trying to kiss the director's butt. That'd be me. Whose butt they're all kissing.

It is fantastic.

"What I don't know, though"—I catch Libby's eyes here, and they are wide like I'm a scary movie with no ending—"is what it's like to be *you*. So, bring what's special about you to your part. Ya know?"

One of the less-bright upperclassman boys shouts, "I just learned how to juggle!" and I'm about to say, "That could be useful!" when Libby butts in with, "Different show, but we love the effort," squeezing my shoulder as if to say, "Was *that* your speech?"

"So let's announce the cast, after that stirring intro from Nate!" Libby exclaims.

I see him again, Ben, fidgeting with his hat and sneaking a couple spare donuts into his bookbag. Frankly, I admire the petty crime. It makes me miss Times Square.

Libby runs through the cast list announcement with such energy that nobody has time to be heart-broken or particularly happy, either.

"The role of Compeyson," Libby says, taking her shoes off and tossing them into the corner of the room, "which is written to be for a man—and is, of course, our main antagonist, a criminal mastermind who leaves Miss Havisham at the altar!—will be played by Rebecca G.! Because screw the patriarchy and girls can be villains too."

Rebecca G. looks stunned, but two of her friends offer her the kind of side-hugs you give someone when you don't want to mess up their hair, and they both go, "You can totally do this, Bec, you've *so* got that mean side to you." And she goes, "Thanks?" and they're still hugging her and not making eye contact.

". . . and the role of Pip's best friend," Libby says, scanning the crowd, "will be played by Jim-Jim Tyers."

Jim-Jim is fun, a junior who is so big that everyone calls him his name twice.

"Why that part?" Jim-Jim says, though not in an aggressive way.

Libby points to me, and I say, "Ah, I'm on! Okay, we thought you're perfect for 'John Wemmick' because he's a clerk in the book, and everyone knows you work at the golf pro shop in the summers at the country club, Jim-Jim."

He looks like he isn't sure what the word *clerk* means.

"Ya know, like . . . an employee at a retail place."

And Jim-Jim pumps a fist and says, "Right on." And you just cannot tell me there's anything more heartening than a group of kids putting on a play without irony. Sorry. Musical.

And just as I'm about to make another announcement—that we're using pop songs for our score, since it's a *tad* too ambitious, even for me, to write an entire musical in three weeks—my Miss Havisham, Paige of the coach lineage, says: "Would anyone mind if I had my mom bring my flute to the next practice?"

Rehearsal, Paige. Rehearsal. Practice is what you

do when you're about to lie to your parents about something.

"I keep hearing this is going to be a musical," she says, "and I'm happy to contribute what I'm able to."

"Yeah, we're actually using pop songs!" I blurt, licking final sugar remnants from my lips. "We'll grab the karaoke tracks online and find perfect songs to correspond to your characters. That's how we're handling the music portion of our musical."

Libby's eyeing me like I've lit her basement on fire, because this was Libby's idea.

"Which was totally Libby's concept!" I add.

"That's right, folks," Libby says, jumping off the coffee table and landing in the arms of a senior. "She isn't just a producer, she's also a visionary."

"So I don't need my flute?" Paige says, and Libby says, "No, Miss Havisham, your hair is enough of a statement," and reaches out to grab Paige's hand.

Libby finishes her casting announcements, right as the last donut is being wolfed down by a junior who doesn't seem too thrilled to have been cast as an understudy.

"Oh! And the part of Arthur Havisham," Libby says, "the bad-boy younger brother, is still being cast."

And that's when Ben sees me seeing him.

I guess I should mention in here that I didn't get the role of Pip—Libby says she wants me fully "focused on directing," not "hogging the spotlight" too. Not that the gym even has a spotlight. Anyway, it's no biggie, and I don't want to focus too hard on that, okay? *Okay??*

"Let's take a five!" I yell, kicking my Keds off, and running barefoot to pee before any actors can corner me with questions or concerns or concerned questions. Or questionable concerns, ha.

A Totally Unbelievable Scene at a Window

Have you ever seen one of those fully unbelievable scenes in a movie in which a boy knocks on the window of a girl?

Knock-knock.

Well, believe it.

It's Ben. Mendoza. Hat wearer, homeroom sharer, rehearsal crasher.

I'm in bed, scrolling through Instagram, deeeeeep into Jordan's profile and feeling queasy, like something's off about all his recent photos, when I hear it—the tapping. The Tapping from Beyond.

Now, true: All of this would be more impressive if we lived in one of those two-floor homes over in Libby's 'hood, but we don't. We have a ranch house. Single-level. But still. It's my window. It's after 10 p.m. Mom thinks I went to bed twenty minutes ago (technically I did!), and let's just say that Ben's profile in the moonlight is something out of a scary movie. One that stars a strangely compelling local boy, the type you'd cast as a background extra, except he keeps showing up in scenes he doesn't belong in.

"Mendoza, what are you doing here?" I whisper-shout after I crack open my window, which takes more effort than it should because I have the upper-body strength of a sleeping fourth-grade girl.

"Did you know we're neighbors?"

I tug my T-shirt down over my boxers.

"What are you talking about?"

"My family moved over here a couple months ago. Or, my mom and me did, I guess."

"You guess?"

"I mean, I know." He's fidgety, and if he raises his voice enough to wake up my dad, a rifle could become accidentally involved (my dad hunts deer, *whee*).

"I'm not inviting you in, because that would be odd."

"Cool, yeah, no—I just wanted to say I'm sorry for coming to your rehearsal uninvited."

I cross my arms. "How was the donut you stole when you thought nobody was looking, Mendoza?"

"The donu—oh, you saw me take it?"

"A director notices everything," I say, basically channeling Libby, who would *d-i-e* die to have a cute boy show up at her window.

I have decided Ben is cute.

"Yeah, so, I obviously missed your auditions—I was mowing lawns for cash—but I was sort of curious about maybe, like, if all the parts were cast?"

Now I want a donut, by the way. You say the word *donut* and it's like a promise.

I hear the quietest footfalls ever, from behind me in the hallway. My mom is so skinny she's like half sparrow, these days, a lady who never quite finishes any dish.

"What's wron—" Ben starts.

I make the *shh* sign, and then mouth, "My mom."

"Okay," he murmurs back. An okay that could mean literally anything.

I pull my T-shirt down again and whisper, "Seriously, though, let's talk about this in homeroom tomorrow," and start to shut the window.

He jams his hand into the frame to stop me. People on the subways back in New York used to do this, and hold everybody up, stopping the train from leaving the station on time.

But oddly, I don't feel held up here.

"If there's any parts at all," Ben goes, "I'm always on the hunt for extra credit in English class. I, um, don't read so good. Ta-da: Dyslexia is fun! Or write so good either. So *well*, I should say. Ha-ha."

"I thought you were Mr. English's star student."

"Nah, that dude grades on the meanest curve! I still only have a B-plus, and I work my butt off in his class!"

What I'd give for a B-anything to be considered *not* good enough.

I squat down and talk through the window crack. "Have you ever acted in anything before?"

"I mean, just now I told my mom I was running out to get her a liter of Diet Coke. So, yeah, I'd say I'm pretty good at drama."

He is funny, this Ben. Funny in a not-funny way that creeps back around and is funny.

"So, wait, you lied to come over here?"

"I mean, whatever," he says, and there's a weird flash that happens in his eyes. I can see he's a kid who gets in trouble for getting angry. And in that moment I see myself in him, because I'm a kid who gets in trouble for never fighting back. For hiding.

"Hold up," I say, opening the window again. "The 7-Eleven is like a mile away. Your mom makes you go out after ten at night for Diet Coke?"

"No worries, I have my bike," he says, lifting handlebars away from the side of my house. He has his bike, like that's an excuse for going out after ten for Diet Coke, when you're fourteen. For your mom. On a Tuesday.

Maybe I have a good mom after all.

"And it's only point-seven miles," Ben says, holding up his phone to show me the distance logged. "It's on the way to school. I ride there most days. And my mom's kinda laid up with a thing. It's no big deal. Diet Coke makes her happy, and believe me, it's better when she's happy."

His face makes me believe him.

He takes his baseball hat off and runs his hands through his hair, which has a single streak of faded purple dye, I notice for the first time. And he goes, "So, Foster, whaddya say?"

I'm stirred up and shaky suddenly, like I was on opening night of *E.T.*

"I'll think about it," I say, because I hear my mom's sparrow steps out in the hall, again, up to turn on the TV, late, to catch the end of the news and doze off and probably avoid my dad till he's asleep himself.

Ben does his version of a smile, which is basically just a twitch, and he turns away, and I am surprised to watch him strap on a helmet, *click*. I can think of seven adjectives about this kid before I'd say "safety-conscious," but Ben is a surprise.

"Well, no matter what, I'm coming to rehearsal next Saturday."

Bold. Which I'd usually like. My whole life I'm trying to be as bold as the nearest bold person. But tonight I'm annoyed. Annoyed or maybe just ratcheted up a notch. I mean, it's an unbelievable scene to have a boy knock on your window.

"Well, what if I don't cast you?"

"Then I'll be in the crew, or whatever—I'll run out and get you Diet Coke liters." He tightens his helmet's strap. "I just want to get out of the house, Nate. Give me somewhere to go."

My mom knocks on my door and when I look back to wave at Ben, all I see are little flashes of safety tape, glinting in the bicycle moonlight.

"One sec," I say to my mom. I'm opening Instagram to follow Ben before I forget, but Jordan's profile is up, from ten minutes ago. "One more sec, Ma."

And bam, I realize what seemed off about Jordan's pictures. Why I was feeling so queasy, earlier, going deeeeeep into Jordan's profile.

He's erased all the photos of us.

Here Comes the Bride

I can see her coming for me, down the hall, carrying her flute case like a weapon. She's like a lion on the savannah, and I, her acne-prone prey.

It's Paige, and she's cornering me directly after I exit physical chemistry class.

"Are you in director mode or student mode?" she says, her neon braces hypnotizing me. Really, I'm in physical chemistry mode, a.k.a. a sex ed daze.

In that class, they spend a *lot* of time instructing us how to not get people pregnant—but *not* a lot of time telling us what to do if you are a boy who used to have a thing with another boy, and formerly texted him thirty times a day, and *now* second-guess yourself if you even want to send him something innocent, like the lightning-bolt emoji. Or, something less innocent, like: "why in the name of musical theater would you erase all the amazing photos of us on instagram??"

"I'm . . . in Nate mode," I finally say to Paige. "I'm a director, I'm a peer, I'm whatever you need."

She nods a bunch, and says, "I just had a question about Miss Havisham? The character I'm playing?"

"Yep, I'm aware."

Paige balances against a locker, unzips her way-too-big bookbag, and pulls out photos from a wedding that looks to have occurred sometime between the years 1910 and 1980. Hard to say.

"*That* is my beautiful mom," Paige says, pointing to a shot of a woman who looks stunned to be at her own wedding, her hair crimped and primped for days, her makeup applied by a team of clowns.

"What a look!" I say.

"I know!"

Paige then "walks her fingers" over the photo to point to a beefy guy, two people down from her mom, standing under a mighty oak tree and fake-grinning. "And *that*, if you can believe it, is the gym coach. My mom's brother."

My eyes cartoon–bug out and practically make a *Boing!* sound, because it's challenging to believe the coach was ever *anywhere* in the vicinity of—dare I say—attractive. But pictures don't lie.

"What a *look*!" I say again.

"Anyway, my question!" Paige says, handing me

the photo, and giving off the faintest whiff of Funyons and yellow Starbursts.

"I'm all ears," I say. And nose.

"Since Miss Havisham is nuts," Paige says, talking double-time, "and goes around wearing the wedding dress from the time she was stood up at the altar—and since *I* happen to *fit* into my mom's wedding dress— well, Mr. Director, do you see where this is going?"

I . . . don't. "Of course," I say, because, as a director, you can never let your cast lose confidence in you.

"Okay, cool beans. So that settles it: I'm going to *force* my mom to let me wear her wedding dress for the day of the show." Paige takes the photo back and hops exactly once. "You're the Natest, Nate!"

"Thanks."

And then Paige makes the Star Trek symbol with her hand—the nerdiest stage manager from *E.T.* used to do this too, as both a hello and a goodbye; the dork's version of "Aloha." And so I make the symbol to Paige too.

And that's it. She skips away, releasing her prey back into the wild.

"Yo, Paige," I say, and she flips back around like she's in trouble, or has toilet paper stuck to her shoe, or some nonsense. "Thanks for caring about the show so much."

She grins. From a distance, you actually can't see her braces at all. "Of course. The show is the best."

I Guess This Is a Thing Now

For years my parents have been royally terrible at the art of sleeping.

My mom is up all hours of the night, pacing, like she's haunted, a ghost with an unnamed grudge. And maybe the grudge is that my dad likes to fall asleep in bed watching Fox News, late, willing himself awake with caffeine. And all my mom wants is some good sleep.

But they're not me.

Like, my one special skill is I can conk out anywhere—a bus, a futon, a bad movie. The only place I've ever not nodded off is at a musical, because duh.

I sleep both really well and really late and I hope that never changes.

"Natey, you're up so early."

But it's another Saturday morning, before our

second-ever rehearsal for my project, and I've been awake for hours.

"Mom, it's ten."

"You usually sleep till ten-thirty."

"Yeah, I guess I have a lot on my mind."

I'm sitting in front of a bowl of generic alphabet cereal, moving the letters around to spell something, or see a message. I haven't heard from Jordan in a couple days and I'm pushing my spoon into the mush and asking it questions. Like it's a soggy Ouija board.

Does Jordan still like me? I'm think-asking it. But all I'm getting back is vowels. An *o*, and an *e*. Three *a*'s. Nothing conclusive.

Mom puts down a glass of Sunny D, and before I say, "I don't drink my calories anymore!" she says, "I don't want this to go to waste and you're the only reason I bought it."

So I gulp it down and man, it's good.

"Got something on your mind?" she says, and I say, "Nah," but then right away, "I guess I'm just worried I bit off more than I can chew with the *Great Expectations* project."

She goes to do that parent-thing where they kind of ruffle your hair like you're a dog, but at the last minute she swerves, and bends down, and gives Feather a pat instead.

"If anyone can put on a show, it's you, Natey," she says, and it's really sweet.

My dad shuffles out from their bedroom, mumbles, "*Oh*," like he genuinely forgot he had a family, and turns back around.

"You know how to put on a show, Natey," Mom says, ignoring him. "So go put on a show."

Out of the corner of the window I see Ben in my front yard, on his bike, and my face twitch-smiles. I guess he's taking me to rehearsal. I guess this is a thing now.

Acting Is About Channeling Crappy Stuff from Your Past

"Remember, the character is only seven years old in the first scene, so you may want to pitch your voice into a higher place."

I'm offering this wisdom to the boy playing Pip, who is objectively terrible and doesn't have the range and Libby cast him over me, but whatever. I have to focus on directing.

"Seven is literally half my age!" he says.

"Literally, yes," I say, and turn to a girl I've empowered as a stage manager. "Can you hit the lights? We're in a graveyard here, folks!"

So she cuts out all the lights in Libby's basement, but it only gets half-dark. Maybe I'm scrunching up my face like I'm not happy, because the boy who plays Pip says, "Do you want me to run home and get these, like, heavy blankets my dad keeps in the trunk for hunting? I can tape them up to the windows and it'll get super dark in here. If it'll help."

I put my hand on his shoulder and say, "Nah."

Paige is in the corner murmuring her lines, all from the highlighted dialogue in her torn and worn *Great Expectations* from school, and I like this. A lot. Gimme an actor who practices without being prodded! Point: Paige.

Is she a natural for Miss Havisham? That's a big nope, a blinking nope, neon like her braces. But I'm stuck with her, and I'm trying to focus on the positive. Like, how she always brings me a Rice Krispies treat before rehearsal.

"Okay," I say to the room. "Let's go to the top of the scene. Does everyone have their copy of the novel?" I don't wait for them to answer. "Great. So, you're in a graveyard, Pip. You're visiting your parents and sibling, whose headstones we will someday have when the props department pulls it together. And you meet an escaped convict."

A sophomore girl, named Lisa but referred to (behind her back) as Mona Lisa because nobody's ever seen her smile, steps in. She's tough as heck and a perfect convict, and I loved casting a girl as a burglar, even though statistically guys always get into worse stuff and are basically idiots. In my experience.

"Can I ask a question?" Pip dares to say.

"Sure," I say, and I catch myself getting the tiniest bit short with him.

"I guess I'm just, like, super lucky that I've never lost anyone, in real life? So, here I am at a graveyard, and I'm wondering how to pretend to be sad?"

Whoa! There I go, somehow up on my feet, kind of springing around. "Okay, I love this!"

Libby appears at the top of the steps to check on rehearsals. Let's be honest, to check in on me.

"Teachable moment!" I say, trying to ignore her. She's my toughest, truest critic.

A few of the cast drop their phones for a sec and I decide to give 'em the tiniest master class.

"Acting is about channeling crappy stuff from your past."

A girl who is sad to not have a leading part nods too hard.

"Otherwise, it's just crappy stuff, it's just gunk. It doesn't have a bigger purpose."

I can literally feel Libby frowning at me, as if I'm eating up valuable rehearsal time. I look to get a visual. Def a frown.

"So, what you do is"—I look right at Pip—"you name something super bad that happened to you once."

I pause. He gives me *like, right now?* eyebrows, and I give him *duh* eyebrows back.

"I mean, I asked for a new gaming console for Christmas, and didn't get it?" Scattered laughter. His face lights up—everyone loves to land a laugh. But he wasn't kidding, folks.

"Perf! Seriously, perf. But go deeper. Like give me a *loss*."

Pip goes blank-faced like a big white dressing-room wall that needs decorations.

"Oh!" (This, from my female convict.) "I have an uncle who accidentally broke his neck at Mount Rushmore."

This is what I'm working with.

"Thanks for that, Lisa. Pip, does that inspire anything in you?"

Mount Rushmore seems to stir Pip. "Okay, I got something—my cousin got a weird disease and they could never find a diagnosis."

"And?"

"And?"

"What's the end of the story?"

I hear Libby's stairs creak, and she turns and exits. I'm telling myself it's an "Okay, Nate's got rehearsals under control" exit, and not a "Nate is a disaster of a director and I cannot watch this train wreck" exit.

And that's when I hear it. Or actually, *feel* it, first. The room tenses up, all eyes on Pip, who is whimpering.

"S-sorry," he says.

"Is this about your cousin?" I say.

"Yeah, but she's good! She's actually alive and fine now! It was just crappy for a while. I haven't thought about it in years."

"It's all good, man," says Jim-Jim, blessed Jim-Jim, so big that anything he approves receives over half the room's blessing, automatically, since he takes up over half the room.

Mona Lisa puts her hand on Pip's shoulder, which is cool, but I'm not having it. If an actor's crying, I'm using it.

"You're at a gravesite!" I say, to get the scene back up and running. "You're visiting your dead family, you've got a British accent—and *boo!* A convict appears . . ."

Pip sniffs twice, laughs at what it looks like to be a boy, crying—I wish all my fellow boys would just get over it and cry like three times as often; it's very cleansing/good for your skin—and shakes it off. Mona Lisa squeezes his shoulder and runs back to her place at the top of the scene, and the stage manager stands in front of the window, to get the room darker.

"Now," I say, "*go.*"

If You Give an Adult Enough Chances

Sometimes you have to corner an adult and demand to know exactly what's going to stand between you and an A+. Like, let's cut the nice stuff and be real, right?

After English class the following Monday, I ask Mr. English if I can have five minutes.

"And cut into my precious internet time?" he says, and I can't tell if he's kidding. Free tip: Five minutes is a good unit of time for adults because in theory it shouldn't overwhelm them; it's just five minutes.

"I mean," I say, tugging my bookbag strap as a makeshift security blanket, "I guess I could come back during lunch?"

"It's fine."

I perch on top of one of the desks, and am kind of silent, and then I remember that I asked *him* for the meeting.

"Oh!" I say.

"Oh."

"So, what's your favorite music?"

He looks at me harsh, like I'm the sun except not bright. His lips sputter trying to form thoughts, then words. "In what context, Mr. Foster?"

"Like, we're choosing pop songs for our musical and I want to get a good grade, so I want to give you what you want. Song-wise." A pause. "Since you're grading."

He grunts and it turns into a snort. He pulls out an energy bar and undoes the wrapper and puts his feet up on his desk.

"Do you drive your parents crazy?" he says mid-bite.

"Excuse me?"

"No, it's just: Precocious students—my most precocious students throughout the years—their parents always seem surprised when I say that despite their getting a D in my class, they're among my most entertaining students."

"Wait, I'm getting a D?"

He swallows too big a piece of the energy bar and hacks for a sec, and I wonder if I'm going to watch Mr. English die before he can change my grade to something better.

"Never mind," he says. "I'm just saying I get a kick out of you, in spite of you."

"Thank you?"

"None necessary," he says, standing to indicate he's either still choking and needs help, or this meeting is over. "It wasn't by definition a compliment. More of an observation."

I hop up, turn toward the bulletin board, notice it isn't decorated at all. Mr. English has been around so long he doesn't even bother with things like decorating the bulletin board. I have to respect that, the same way I came home and took down all my old Broadway posters because now that I've actually *been* on Broadway, it's just a lot to be surrounded by your job, at home.

"Have a decent afternoon," he says when I'm apparently just standing in the middle of the room.

"You too," I say, and start walking toward the empty bulletin board, and the exit.

And then, quietly, I hear a sigh, and: "Elvis, Simon and Garfunkel, and Joni Mitchell."

I turn around.

"Is that," I say, "like, a law firm?"

His jaw clenches and he's got a mad-dad look, but then he laughs and rubs his eyes. "No. They're my favorite singers. Per your request."

I tap my hand on the doorframe. An in!

"See if you can work them into your outrageous

musical project thing, which will be due before you know it."

I'm about to correct him—it's a *musical*, not a play—but he got the terminology right this time.

If you give an adult enough chances, they can actually learn.

You Can't Tap-Dance to a Ballad

"This music is sloooooowwwww," Libby says. "The sixties were just ballad city."

She's in her bedroom and so am I, even though we've crossed the critical age when most moms don't let a boy and a girl hang out alone with a door shut. But Libby's mom isn't like most moms, and let's be honest. I'm not like the other boys. Sometimes I feel like I'm three life choices away from having a signature wig line.

"No, this music could be so good!" I say, mostly to convince myself, and trying not to yawn at all the acoustic guitar strumming.

We're streaming Mr. English's songs and trying to imagine a good place for them in the show, but the best place for them would be far underground, in a coffin. "Seriously, we can make these work."

"Uh, mm'kay," Libby says, "so you're confident

that the story of a crazy old British lady will pair well with your grandparents' folk songs?" She produces, from her pocket, a temporary tattoo, and proceeds to hunt for a place to put it on her forearm.

"What I'm saying is I want Mr. English to give me a good grade."

"Then maybe you shouldn't have cast the gym coach's niece. Paige's voice sounds like a cat on a piano."

"What if—wait, what if we just have everyone lip-sync the original songs?"

I jump up.

It sounded good in my head, and unlike most of my ideas, when I said it out loud, it still sounded good.

"Like, we've got this awesome sound system in the gym. And these songs that Mr. English loves. What if we just have the cast lip-sync the songs, and it's up to me to make sure the song makes sense in the plot?"

Libby licks her forearm and slams the tattoo down, right over a place where she's got a tricky mole she hates and is always looking for ways to cover it. She does all of this without breaking eye contact with me, by the way. "Intriguing," she says, and then looks at her iPhone, which we're using to DJ tonight's song stream. "Okay, pop-quiz time."

I kerplop back down on a beanbag chair that long ago lost its oomph.

"Can't help falling in love," Libby says, and I go: "Are you—wait—am I helping write a text exchange with a boy for you?" and she goes, "Noooo, it's an Elvis song. 1961. 'Can't Help Falling in Love.'"

"What about it?" I'm lightly punching the beanbag chair.

"Find a place for it in *Great Expectations*. You've got ten seconds. Ten, nine . . ."

I throw my head back into the beanbag nothingness and look up at Libby's ceiling, to a poster from a flop musical production of *Breakfast at Tiffany's* that we used to throw our bubblegum at, just to try and make it stick. It's a good poster to lose your thoughts in.

"The marriage scene at the end of the book!" I say, and I actually snap my fingers like we're in a movie, which we're not. We're in Jankburg, PA. As cinematic as it sounds. "When Pip stands at the altar. He can sing 'Can't Help Falling in Love' and we can do a big tap dance."

"It's a ballad, genius." She blows on her tattoo to dry it. "You're gonna have the cast *tap*-dance? To an Elvis ballad?"

"Then we'll do a waltz! Work with me here."

"Okay, fine. We've got one song down."

She holds her tattooed arm up for approval.

"Love it," I say. "Never change."

"Flattery will get you everywhere. Okay: 'Jailhouse Rock.'"

"Easy. The Act One closing number. Prison reform is a giant theme in *Great Expectations*."

"How do you know, you only got ten pages in."

"I read the complete and entire SparkNotes twice."

She laughs.

"Next: 'Scarborough Fair,' a.k.a. 'Parsley, Sage, Rosemary, and Thyme.'"

"Now you're just making me hungry."

"C'mon, it's a Simon and, let's see, *Garfinkel* song. Find a place for it, because I'm still not convinced this is the right ide—"

"The Christmas dinner scene!" I yell. "When Pip comes back with the stuff that Mona Lisa the convict convinces him to steal."

I dance around a little. I'm on fire.

"What does any of that have to do with a series of four spices?"

"Somebody can be like, *This recipe is delicious*, and Pip can be like, *Thanks, the secret is a pinch of thyme, plus a little rosemary, and a big serving of parsley*."

This makes Libby chuckle so hard that she hits her head on a shelf. "The pain is worth it. Your insane idea about using these folk songs for our musical just might actually work."

"Yes, yes, yes!" I yell, and punch right through the beanbag chair fabric, spilling Styrofoam balls everywhere.

"Welp," Libby says, not even getting up. Just watching as the beanbag chair expels its insides all over the floor. "I've hated that chair for a while now and I am insulted it's not filled with actual beans. You're a liar, bean chair."

"I am so, so sorry," I say, trying to pick up the tiny balls as they scatter every which way and disappear into Libby's old carpet.

"Don't be," she says, turning her phone around to show me the screen. "Just know that we've picked a grand total of three songs, and we need about another fifteen, and we open in two and one-half weeks."

My own phone goes off, my ringtone for Jordan: a medley from *Dreamgirls* that I ripped from online.

"Uh, excuse me," Libby says, "we're supposed to be on airplane mode."

I hold up the screen to show her who it is.

"Ew," she says. "You drew hearts on his contact photo."

I giggle-sigh and shush her and pick up. "Jordy! I'm with Libby! We just had a really good music idea for my show!"

But he's not interested in my really good music idea for my show, or my anything.

Instead, he tells me "how much money!!" he's making on *his* show. His TV show. Which does not take place in a high school gym.

"No way. Wow. That's a lot of money."

Libby rolls her eyes, leaves the room, and comes back with more temporary tattoos from the crafts closet in the basement. Giving me enough time to ask Jordan why he erased all the photos of us on Instagram—"not to make this awkward"—and enough time for him to pretend like he had to get back to set before he could answer—"what a terrible time for me to be pulled back to work!"

And we hang up without saying goodbye.

"You know, isn't that just life," Libby says, taking my phone and hiding it under her mattress. "You have one good moment, one great breakthrough on your ridiculous project, and then a dumb boy comes along and makes you feel small again."

I choose a dragon tattoo, and wonder if putting it on my neck would seem like a cry for help or an edgy new definition of myself. Every other day, these days, I just want to start over as the kind of boy who likes dragons just 'cause they're dragons, and not because they're friends with unicorns.

"He's making a lot of money, Lib."

"Tell me. No, wait, don't tell me."

She chooses a butterfly in a leather jacket and holds it up to her forehead.

"Boys are the worst," I say, and Libby says, "Amen, sister."

And then, the way best friends do, we read each other's minds and don't even put on the tattoos.

We just go downstairs for a snack break that turns into a second dinner that turns into an accidental burping contest. Libby wins, and I head out to her yard.

"Since when did you start riding a bike?" Libby says from her doorway, after my snack/second-dinner combo settles down a bit.

"I dunno. Ben sort of got me into it." I don't blink. Libby smirks.

I don't tell her that Ben promised to teach me how to skateboard or that I promised to teach him how to dance.

"So you *do* know," she says, but I'm already pedaling off, and thinking how my mom should probably make a bigger deal out of me not wearing a helmet.

At the stop sign I turn back around. Libby's in her front yard practicing her splits. When you're fourteen, you're basically sixteen but also basically twelve.

"Do you think Paige is actually terrible in the

show?" I ask, and Libby says, "Did *Hamilton* deserve to sweep every Tony category?"

I'm confused because actually, yes, I genuinely think it did? But Libby likes going against the grain, on purpose, so I take it that she disagreed with *Hamilton*'s lighting design Tony or something.

"What am I going to do about her?" I say. Libby looks up at the night clouds for an answer, and comes right back with, "Give her a bunch of Joni Mitchell songs. Mr. English is a dad. Dads always like Joni Mitchell, if my dad is any indication."

"Solid."

"Duh."

I ride home, my mind a fuzz of food and Ben, and it's the perfect temperature out, which only happens like three nights a year in Jankburg. I don't break a sweat, but I'm definitely out of breath enough to count it as solid exercise.

Maybe I'll be the kind of high schooler who exercises. Yeah. Maybe.

I walk into the kitchen and say hi to my mom, and I eat an entire sleeve of butter crackers and ask where Dad is, not for any good reason, just 'cause. And Mom goes, "Who knows," and gets up and does the one dish that's in the sink.

Not Like an Ocean or Something Pretty

What would we do without water fountains to fake-pass the time?

I'm in gym class (I know, ugh), the next day. (Seriously, pity me. I'll wait.) And during my fourth water break in twenty minutes, the coach must catch onto me avoiding any exertion, because he blows a whistle and says, "*Foster*, get in here."

I take one more epic and truly long sip of water, until my stomach autofills with pee, and then I blurt out to the coach: "I'll have to make this quick, because I am about to actually use my shorts as a bathroom otherwise."

He bounces a half-inflated soccer ball against cinderblock office walls that look like the stage manager's room back in New York.

"It'll be quick," he goes, not bothering to look at me.

Typical. Male. Adult.

"Am I—wait, am I in trouble for missing seventeen hoops in a row? Because, the hoops are so high and I am so short."

He catches the soccer ball in his yard-wide meat hand and spits something into his wastebasket.

"No, I don't care," he says. When we actually make eye contact, he mumbles a little and then goes, "I was just going to thank you. My niece is having the time of her life in your English project skit. Says you and the Elizabeth girl—"

"Libby," I half say, and he gets the dad-look where he hates being interrupted, so I make the son-sign of *Sorry, I'll shut up, go on.*

"And that you're both making her feel very welcome, and like she's doing a not-bad job."

A kid runs into the coach's office and says, "Coach, Mindy has a nosebleed," and the coach stays in his seat for one second too long and goes, "Okay, tell her to go to the nurse." My bladder is beating in time with my heart. It's a real medical achievement.

"So, there," he says.

"Anything else, coach?"

"Nobody's been nice to Paige since she was a little kid, so I appreciate it, is all. The *band* kids aren't even cool with her. She's gone through a lot and I appreciate it." His eyes are liquid, not like an ocean or something pretty, more like a rough suburban swimming pool, and he goes, "Now get the heck outta here."

Some Days

Some days, unlike most days, you wake up and your head isn't heavy, and when you swing your feet out from under your covers, they find your slippers without you even having to look down.

In other words, some days it all comes together.

Some days you don't step on any cracks on the sidewalks, your teachers leave you alone, and there's a fire drill during a social studies quiz.

Some days—not most days, but some of them—your cast of actors high-fives you in the hallways, and a few of the teachers stop you, to say they hear you've got something "special on your hands, Mr. Foster" (their words; this happened literally twice today).

Some days the coach tells you that you can just "skip gym class this semester as long as you go work quietly in the library." I'm telling you, this actually happened.

Jim-Jim pulls me aside later, by the trophy case in the entry hall at school, and says, "What do you think?"

And I'm like *Of what?* with my face.

So he goes, "Of my costume!"

I remember then that I'd asked the cast to wear their costumes to school today, so I can approve them or offer . . . feedback. And Jim-Jim looks pretty good: khakis that nearly fit (the kid grows an inch a week, so he's showing a *lot* of sock), and a neutral hoodie that's made of like a brown knit material, that looks kind of generically old-fashioney. I ask him if he's willing to take his earring out for the day of the show, and he's like, *duh*.

Then Ben walks by at the same moment, and goes, "Ta-da!" Except the thing is, I don't love Ben's outfit—"I don't think there were light blue jeans back then in *Great Expectations* days," I'm forced to say. But I know the kid has a rough home life. And so some days, you make a plan with a cute boy to stop by the nearly deserted mall after school, because you've got a gift card from your aunt to a department store, so how about you buy him some pants? Just for the show.

Like, this is just a professional work obligation. It's not even an official hangout.

Anyhoo, some days you're a freshman in high

school, and though the world is a bubble of suck, inside the bubble you've made something rare and beautiful. The downside being: At any moment it could collapse.

Jordan calls me while Ben is in the fitting room in the men's room at American Eagle. Ben comes out to show off a little, but none of the pants really work on him. He's got kind of strange (but cute) legs that are short but paired with a long (and cute) upper body, which I swear I'd never noticed before this.

The semi-helpful checkout lady—a mom-type working at the mall while her kid is at college, I bet—offers to find Ben "the exact right pants," and then calls him "sir," which makes us laugh. He's thirsty after biking over here from school, says he's going to go get a Coke, and asks if I want anything, but I'm like, *Nah*.

But I'm checking my texts, and Jordan's sent a bunch of "why aren't you picking up?"s when I hear Ben yell, "Diet Root Beer?" from outside the store, and I shout back: "How did you know I love that stuff?" and he goes, "I know things," and smirks, and it's a pretty good moment.

My hand vibrates, or my phone does in it, I should say. So this time I pull myself into the girls' short-shorts section, and pick up—just in case Jordan has, like, an emergency hernia or something. "Jordy," I say over FaceTime, "whaddup."

"I hear your musical is amazing. Like it's literally gotten back to me on the set."

"You're kidding, how?"

"Details, details," he says. "Just a sec!" he yells off-camera. "Interview," he explains with an eye roll.

"I'd love to be interviewed for something," I say. "Sounds genuinely and not ironically fun."

"It's overrated, and all your stories are canned beforehand. Like, the publicist made me *memorize* a funny story. It's all fake to promote the project."

Ben's already back, or almost back; I see him, across the corridor that American Eagle shares with an Auntie Anne's Pretzels, doing my entire cast's inside-joke dance move, just to make me laugh.

He hauls our giant drinks back across the corridor, toward me, and Jordan goes, "What's so funny?"

But I do a *You wouldn't get it* shake of my head.

Because I've got a whole other kind of humor with Ben.

With Ben, I'm goofy, I'm a leader, I'm the person giving him the answers. We giggle at stupid stuff.

With Jordan I'm the understudy who's lucky if the lead calls out of work sick.

It's a dynamic we never totally got used to, or recovered from. If Jordan was at work, he was onstage. If I was onstage playing *his* part, he was home.

"C'mon, tell me," Jordan says, at the same time

that Ben swears a pretty bad word, and spills his Coke all over the girls' fake-fur hoodies at the front of the store, which should buy me a second.

And so for reasons I can't explain, I get up the courage to say something I've never said to Jordan.

"Jordan—" Here goes. I'm going to ask him if he loves me. Crazy, right? I'm feeling crazy. Or like I have to know. "Do you—"

"Hold that thought. Listen: My manager's nephew's college roommate still lives in Pittsburgh."

"Wait, is this story going to involve math? I'm already confused."

I hate family trees, because when I tried to do mine for a sixth-grade project, I discovered that my parents were so deeply incurious about their own pasts that I ended up telling half the class I was related to royalty and the other half I was an adopted orphan.

"The *point* about my manager's nephew's college guy," Jordan says—rare, a Jordan story with a point!— "is that he's a producer, did some stuff for the Pittsburgh Cultural Trust, once helped get Patti LuPone to do a very famous concert downtown, before you were born."

As if Jordan and I aren't the same age, by the way. "Okay?"

"And I'm sending him to see your show. That's how good I heard it is."

"Wait," I say. "So many things."

The nice lady in the store is helping Ben sop up the spilled soda. Ben is the type of kid who sticks around to help people.

I glance at one of those human-length clothing-store mirrors and realize I don't hate my outfit, for once. Usually I hate at least three things about myself. "Where are you hearing my show is so good?"

"Some of your cast are posting videos and, like, live-streaming rehearsals," he explains.

It's Ben. It's Ben who's doing this, I know this, because he wants to maybe be a cinematographer when he grows up, he told me. But I cover, to Jordan, with: "And I don't know about this!"

"Well, you're busy being a fancy-pants director," Jordan says, just as the helper-lady is taking another load of pants off to the dressing room Ben was using.

"Your friend is just helping me mop up the spill," she says to me in passing. "I said, *You don't have to!* But he insisted."

"What friend?" Jordan says. "Are you . . . in a women's clothing section? If you're doing drag without me, I'll kill you."

I look at my outfit again and *poof!* Like an insane person, I realize I actually hate my hair, and that my shoes are like a billion years old.

"A kid from school. From English. From my English class."

Jordan side-eyes me, turns to address somebody off-screen, and says, "As always, I gotta run. Anyway, was just trying to share a compliment! That's the only reason I called!"

Ben is back. He hands me my drink. "Sorry it's all sticky," he says. "There was an incident."

I'm not thirsty at all, but I'm definitely hungry. Maybe a Food Court stop is in order.

"The pants fairy arrived!" he says, leading me back to the changing room.

I murmur, "Hey, who are you calling a pants fairy," but he's already in there, trying on another pair, and doesn't hear me.

He swings the door back open and steps out. "I think these are the ones."

Maverick Boys

It's the kind of Friday night where I just want to have Netflix on in the background while I'm watching live Idina Menzel concert videos on my phone, but that's not the Friday night it ends up being.

Instead Libby invites me over with a cryptic text: "come over now don't ask questions"

And nineteen minutes later: "Eat one of these, trust me," Libby says after I arrive breathless and curious. She sets down my favorite food group (lemon squares) on a tray, and she doesn't even make a fuss or give a warning about not getting powdered sugar on her rug. Because that's the kind of mom she has. Chill.

"Why do I feel like you're about to deliver bad news?" I say, but she's silent and puts down a hot cocoa next to the lemon square, and my stomach is in a civil war of tension and desire.

"Here," she says, and holds her phone up in front of my face. "Watch this."

"An . . . ad for a new car?"

"Ugh, hold on," she says, and skips the ad, and then I see it.

"Jordan," I say. Or, I see *him*, I should say. Though lately, he's been feeling like more of an it than a him. Like a faraway concept instead of an actual verifiable thing, like how nobody knows if the Aurora Borealis is even real.

"Wait for it," Libby says.

He's sitting for the interview that he was prepping for earlier. I know right away because he's in the shirt he was wearing when he and I FaceTimed at the mall, right before Ben found the perfect pants.

"So, congrats on making your TV debut," the host says to Jordan. Who looks so comfortable and bright.

"It's such a blast!" he says, which makes the audience laugh as if it was funny. *"There's so much free food on set!"*

And he pats his stomach like he's Santa even though he has the metabolism of a rabbit.

I reach out and eat an entire lemon square in two bites.

"Yeah, you've really let yourself go, I can tell," the host says, and the audience cracks up like there's a giant blinking sign that says L-A-U-G-H, which there probably is.

"*Anyway, I got my start in the theater, but it's so fun to get a second shot at a hard scene,*" Jordan says, and the host goes, "*I don't get it, what do you mean,*" and Jordan says, "*On Broadway, you only get to do it once and the scene just moves on. On 'Mav'—sorry, 'Maverick Boys'*"—the name of the series—"*if the tears don't come, you get to do it over and over again.*"

The host pretends to cry and Jordan improvises and goes, "*Cut! Do it again!*" and Libby and I both snort at the very same time, and a little bit of lemon square gets stuck in my throat.

"*It must be hard, balancing school and work as a thirteen-year-old,*" the host says, and I go, "He's fourteen!" and when Jordan doesn't correct him, Libby pauses the video.

"So . . . that isn't the only lie the kid spouts," she says.

I burn my tongue on cocoa and Libby hits Play again.

"*Well, yeah,*" Jordan says, swallowing hard. "*Honestly, my big secret is that my girlfriend lets me copy her homework.*"

Actually, no. All he gets out is: "*My girlfriend lets me copy her home—*"

And then the video stops, buffering, caught in Jordan's lie.

The spinny wheel of death just turns and turns,

gripping my chest shut like a vise, and Libby and I are as quiet as quiet gets.

I'm still choking on the lemon square, and my tongue is still throbbing with burnt-ness, when Jordan texts me: "so did you get my voicemail??"

Which is . . . new. We never leave voicemails for each other. What are we, thirty? I open up my mailbox and see his three-minute-long message, and press Play and then Speaker.

"Before you see the interview I just gave," he's saying, fast as heck, "just in case it goes viral or it posted online before we FaceTime: I *just* want to warn you that I say a *mild* white lie in it. Which my agent insisted I say! And . . . like, it's not personal at all. And . . . just call me back so I can explain! Oh, it's Jordy, by the way. Okay. I guess I just hang up? It's been literally six months since I've called someone. There's actually a rule on-set that we're not allowed to speak on our phones! There are so many rules at a TV show, you literally wouldn't believe it. It's like: Are you kidding me? Anyway. Okay, FaceTime me. Bye."

And then it's muffled, but it takes the kid like twenty seconds to figure out how to hang up, and there is swearing involved. Finally, after a brief silence:

"Text him the middle-finger emoji!" Libby says. "Seriously."

No. Not that one. I'm scrolling through *all* the

emojis, trying to figure out the exact right response—the poop emoji, the broken-heart emoji, maybe a taco just to confuse him. But I power my phone off instead.

"Show me the interview again," I say to Libby. I hear my own voice darken, and I hate it. Like, it's the moment in those superhero movies that my dad randomly loves, when the bad guy gets badder.

"Nope," she says. "No more upsetting video content. You're cut off from everything but lemon squares."

I step off her bed. "I have to pee," I say.

"Are you mad at me, for showing you?"

"No."

"Then why do you seem mad?"

"Because I am mad! Because Jordan is telling people he has a girlfriend. Because I was just erased from his life history, which is so much more interesting than *my* life history, and now doesn't even include me!"

"Well, I'm part of your life history," Libby says, just as I'm slamming the door to her bedroom. (She has her own bathroom attached to her bedroom, and she doesn't even have to share it, if you can believe some kids are that fortunate.)

I turn on Libby's hair dryer because her overhead fan is broken and I hate when girls hear me pee. And when I'm done, I'm seeing my reflection in the toilet water like the world's worst wishing well. And then, whoops, it's raining, or I'm crying.

"Natey," Libby says, soft, through the door, once I've turned the blow dryer off and splashed water through my hair and tried to pull together my look a little bit. (Fail.)

"What."

"My mom has a whole other batch of lemon squares downstairs." She clears her throat the way she always does before she gets louder. (Terrible vocal technique.) "And apparently this batch has a little essence of lime in it too, because Mom is experimenting in the kitchen these days, like she's the Ina Garten of Pennsylvania."

I swing the door open and cross my arms and pout.

"There's that smile I love," Libby says. This time we hug full body-to-body, like the old days. None of this too-cool side-hugging.

"I hate him," I say.

"Nobody likes being erased," she goes.

We rock each other like her room has a breeze, and we're a couple of trees whose only roots are each other, or something.

My Whole Life Is a Word Search

Yeah, it turned into a sleepover, as so many things do when they cross the critical 2 a.m. mark.

And so the next morning before rehearsal, I stop at home to get my water bottle, because I still believe in the power of recycling. It's my *E.T.* bottle, and sometimes I wonder if that looks like showing off, to my cast—who don't even get their own swag for *Great* (which is what we call *Great Expectations* for short, even though I wanted to call it *G.E.* as an homage to *E.T.*).

Mom is in the kitchen hovering over her financial ledger for Flora's Floras, my family's flower shop that specializes in affordable displays for all your funeral needs. Look us up.

"Natey, if I have one piece of advice for you," Mom says as I'm pouring Sunny D into my water bottle— because apparently I do drink my calories when under stress—"it's: Don't ever own a small business."

"Got it," I say.

She closes the book and lays her head down on it.

I run up to my room, two steps at a time, and spritz a respectable amount of Axe all over my T-shirt and pants, and then a little more on my T-shirt, and then a whiff more on my hair to be sure I've covered the bases.

And then I power my phone back on from Libby's place, and you guessed it: Jordan has just texted me a bunch of question marks and then a frowny face and then a sobbing face, all from last night.

And I just can't.

"Mom?" I say, back in the kitchen, a halo of Axe following me.

"It's fine," she says.

"What is?"

"Are you asking if you can sleep over at Libby's again tonight? It's fine. I know her house is more fun than ours."

I pull up the chair that Feather used to chew on as a baby dog. It's so honest and true, what Mom just said, that I don't know how to spin away from it. Some families' houses are just a lot more fun than others'.

"No, I wasn't going to ask that. And this house is plenty chill. You finally got us Netflix and Hulu."

She laughs and sloshes the coffee around in her

mug like it's a fine wine, the way Libby's mom does in their kitchen. My mom doesn't "do" wine anymore, she does cold coffee and Diet Coke by the half gallon. Like Ben's mom, I bet.

My phone buzzes again and Jordan is texting: "I didn't mean to make you feel bad. That's all I can say."

"What is it?" Mom says, and elbows me but in a sweet way.

"I was just going to ask you if Dad has ever, like, hurt your feelings, and how did you forgive him?"

She makes an over-the-top clown face like she's Olaf in *Frozen*—but the stage adaptation, obviously, not the movie. "What are you talking about?" she says. "Are you pulling my chain?"

I instantly regret asking for any version of relationship advice. I can feel and hear my phone ring in my pocket again, the buzzing, and I silence it, fast and nervous. And she catches on to me, I guess. Whenever a boy acts quick like a jackrabbit, he's hiding something.

"Ah, someone special?" she says.

My face skin gets so prickly that maybe I'm growing my first-ever mustache.

"No," I say, "I don't know, maybe, how-do-I . . ." But I trail off, like my whole life is a word search.

"Yeah, your dad hurts my feelings sometimes, but I guess I hurt his too."

"Like on purpose?"

"Nah, just being people." She taps the pen against her books. She's got ink all over her hand. She used to be so pulled together in the old days.

"Natey, is there something you want to tell me?" The way she says it, all angular and consonant-full, sounds translated from German.

Yes, so badly. "Nah."

"You can always tell me anything, as long as it won't give me a heart attack."

She goes to kiss my head, but I pull away, and toss the empty Sunny D bottle into the garbage can, and miss by a half mile. It ricochets against the kitchen counters and almost spins into Feather's tail.

"Can you believe Anthony and me are related?" I say, picking the bottle up, placing it in the recycling bin. "Can you believe we share the same DNA?" That kid can dunk hoops in his sleep, blindfolded.

"I love you both equal," Mom says, in a hoarse morning whisper. And before I leave for rehearsal, she goes, "Drinking your calories again, I see." And I say, "I started realizing I wasn't sure who I was staying in such good shape for," and she grunt-laughs and lifts her mug and says, "Hear-hear," and blows me a kiss, which I catch, because nobody's watching.

I'm on the lawn, on my bike, waiting for Ben, when Mom texts me, "Have a good last rehearsal Natey," and I text her back the thumbs-up emoji, but don't send it yet. Because she's still typing. Typing something new, as a follow-up.

I see the text bubbles pop up, then erase, then bubble again. A classic teen move that Mom has never pulled on me.

But right when a truck passes our house, and makes a huge rumble-rumble sound, Mom texts me the gay freaking pride flag (!!!!!!!!!!!!). And doesn't even follow it up with "whoops autocorrect" or anything.

It just sits there bold and still like a flag that nobody's trying to tear down or mess with.

And when I hear Ben say, "I'm here, let's roll!" I almost drop my phone in the grass.

Bossy Nate Is Bossy

Libby can tell something's up with me. Unfortunately.

Here's the funny thing about having a best friend who knows you basically better than she knows herself: She also knows when you're hiding something.

"Okay, guys," I say to my cast, who are all wearing their ridiculously ill-fitting, half-baked costumes from home. There's so many white T-shirts with the collars torn out, it looks like a production of *The Outsiders*, six months into the run after the wardrobe budget ran out. "Let's take it from the top, and remember to really artic-*you*-late even when you're lip-syncing. Because I want the audience experience to be, like: *Whoa, are they really singing, or is that Peter, Paul, and Millie?*"

"Mary!" someone yells, and I say, "Ex*cuse* me?"

And Libby has to lean up on her tiptoes and say, "The singer's name is Mary, not Millie."

It's the first time Libby's ever had to haunch herself up to say anything to me. In this instant, I realize I've grown. I am now half a head taller than Libby. Something about this leaves me shooketh.

Jim-Jim, who is in charge of music at rehearsals, because he has the best wireless speaker system, casually offers (at the "Places!" call) that he forgot his speakers at home. And I blurt out, "Wait, what?!" and Jim-Jim drops his head and says, "Actually, I loaned them to a senior."

"Citizen?"

"No, like: upperclassmen."

Libby smacks her hands against her thighs. "We're about to have our final run-through, Jim-Jim! This is kind of a pivotal moment!"

But strangely, two of my girls apparently independently travel with high-end wireless speakers—"You never know when you need to have a party," one, whose name I haven't fully committed to memory, offers—and so we're back on track.

"What's up with you?" Libby says when Abigail or maybe Autumn, or Amelie, is syncing the speaker with Jim-Jim's phone, which has the show's playlist downloaded.

"What do you mean, I just want today to go well," I say, and I wince as I gulp back some Sunny D, because I guess I've been chewing on my lip, and cut it open, raw.

"Yeah, something's up with you," she eye-roll mutters, and pulls out a big white notepad from her bookbag.

"Oooh, fresh office supplies!" The best, right? The only good part of any project or school event is the office supplies. You can quote me.

Also, I'm trying to distract Libby from uncovering the pride flag on my phone. The minute I show it to her, it's all she's going to be able to focus on. She's like a cat with a laser when it comes to drama. Frankly, she's like *me* with a laser—laser pointers are just incredibly fun.

I nod at the stage manager, a sophomore girl who ran for class president last year and was voted dead last, but relishes power and yelling at boys (obsessed with her for this). She bellows "Places!" so loudly that Libby's mom sticks her head out from the kitchen window upstairs, to check on us.

Pip takes his place by the fence, and the cutest thing happens: A few people give him fist bumps to psych him up, and another guy even gives him this full-on hug.

Mona Lisa is performing some kind of breathing exercise that involves holding her air in until she almost passes out, then hissing at her flat palm until all the air has run out? I'm not sure—it feels like witchcraft—but I admire the commitment.

And the assistant stage manager, a boy whose whole "gag" is that he's got an old-fashioned name, and wears penny loafers and a bowtie to school, goes around and collects people's cell phones. And nobody puts up a fight.

"I'm waiiiiting," Libby says, but not to them. She's in my ear, leaning over and not up now, because we're sitting on an ancient Ikea sofa that Libby's mom let us move to the backyard for rehearsals. "Is it Jordan? Did he do something even *stupider* since last night?"

And that's the exact moment when I see Ben doing push-ups behind the tree that Libby and I carved our names into, back when we were ten. But we didn't etch NATE <3 LIBBY or LIBBY <3 NATE, we carved NATE + LIBBY <3 RAGTIME—a semi-underrated musical about injustice and the Ford motor company, which received a revival that somehow didn't record a cast album, so did it even happen?

Ben hops up, sees me watching him, and grins, and I look away at nothing, too fast. Fast enough that I hear my neck give a little *crick*.

"Is somebody gonna play the overture, 'cause I'm just standing here being stupid?" Pip says, and I catch Jim-Jim flirting on the sidelines, with Paige. I'm both proud of my frizzy-haired, previously unpopular Paige for this moment of romantic clarity, but also super annoyed. So I clear my voice like an old-timey cartoon: *"A-hem."*

"You better tell me at intermission," Libby says, and I guess that does it—fine, she wore me down, whatever.

Because, at the opening guitar strums of "The Sound of Silence"—an old folky duet by a man named Simon and his friend Garth, that we play when Pip comes out and walks through the graveyard at the top of the show—I hold up my phone for Libby to see. I point to the text exchange with my mom, and when the music lets up, the sound is not of silence but of Libby gasping.

"You told your mom you're g—?!"

"No," I say with a gritted jaw, a haze of Axe lifting off me like summer smog on pavement. "She apparently . . . just . . . figured it out. *I don't know how."*

And I swear a weird wind sweeps through the yard, and knocks over all our cardboard headstones. Carl runs out onto the grass to set them back up, but Pip, bless him, keeps speaking, even as Libby's mom's wind chimes go nuts, *bing-bing-bing.*

"My father's family name being Pirrip," he says, like a disaster—it's like, just wait for the breeze to die down, then talk!—*"and my Christian name Philip, my infant tongue could make of both names nothing longer or*

more explicit than Pip. So, I called myself Pip, and came to be called Pip."

A loud text rings out over the speaker system, and Jim-Jim leaps over a beaming Paige, and grabs his phone out of the head stage manager's hand, and says, "Sorry! Lemme just put this on mute!"

But these are just the background details, folks.

The main show is that Libby is still so shocked that my mom knows I'm gay, that it's up to me alone to say, "Hey, guys? Let's go back to the top, and let's always put our phones on vibrate before we turn them into stage management, and let's *especially* always talk twice as loud. You know the rules, don't make me be Bossy Nate."

Apparently they call me Bossy Nate behind my back, which I should hate but I actually 60-percent love. Because, I don't even like bossing myself around. I don't even feel comfortable choosing what under-wear to wear or cereal to eat. That anyone thinks I'm a boss at anything is . . . novel.

"So, let's try this bad boy again."

I barely nod at the stage manager and she shout-screams, "Places, again!" and I see her get revved up by screaming at a junior boy from the lacrosse team who she recruited as an assistant stagehand.

When I plop back down on the sofa, Libby pulls the old thing we used to do, to make each other laugh:

At the last moment you hold out your hand and your friend sits on your open palm. Kid stuff. For kids.

But funnily enough, it still works, and we laugh, and we start "The Sound of Silence" over again.

Ben is filming the entire final dress rehearsal on his phone.

Ben's always filming stuff on his phone.

It's his hobby and I think it's so he can hide behind the camera like how the character Mark does in *Rent*, a musical in the nineties that my Aunt Heidi once told me was "as big as *Hamilton*, and this was pre-Twitter."

Anyway, Ben's got his phone up, making another little movie. He does this any time he's not onstage—or the patch of grass we're using as our stage today. He isn't much good as Arthur, the rebellious brother. He forgets his lines, he talks over other actors, he is always either too LOUD or too soft. But Ben's like our mascot. He makes funny videos; he brings in homemade cookies; he shows up looking exhausted, like he was up half the night avoiding one of his mom's tirades. Probably because he was.

On Broadway, you can't take videos from the wings. I mean, don't get me wrong—I'm verrrrry grateful for people who shoot bootlegs from the balcony, as most of my show knowledge comes from illegal YouTube bootlegs. But you're supposed to just . . .

not. Live theater is supposed to be live, not captured on a rectangle of metal and glass.

But I don't stop Ben. This isn't Broadway. It's a backyard. I'm finally accepting that this comes with its own niceness.

"I thought that was notably not-terrible," Libby whispers to me, after Pip's first monologue.

"Agree," I say, and pretend to write something down on my own spanking new white notepad, which Libby has set in my lap like the power producer she is.

She scribbles a little pride flag on her own notepad, to tease me, and I say, "Don't even."

I'm not going to go over the next part, because, like it or not, it's *Great Expectations*—even a version that includes a fun up-tempo song called "Free Man in Paris," by Joan Mitchell, which I staged to be sung at a bar. But no matter how many times an adult tells you you'll like an old-times book by the end, there are certain things that are just always going to be a little boring. And Charles Dickens is one of them.

Unless it's *Oliver!* and I'm starring in it five years ago, before my voice changed.

"Ten-minute break!" power girl yells, at intermission.

Libby's mom brings out orange slices, and everyone is allowed to have their phones back for ten minutes. But the best thing is that people just sit around talking and inside-joking, and somebody teases me for my "director voice," which I guess I do when I'm talking. (At least it's not a British accent.)

"Look," I say to Libby as she's picking off tomatoes from her hoagie, and throwing them behind a bush that died three summers ago.

"What?"

"Not what. *Who.* Look at how nobody's on their phones. They're acting like a little family. They'd rather be in person than online."

"Oh, that's 'cause our WiFi is down," she says, "and we have terrible reception in the backyard." But then she sees my slightly cracked face and goes, "J.K., it's because everyone loves each other because theater is a family and Bossy Nate is Dad. Duh."

I take a bite of hoagie and it's so good. Sandwiches just get a lot of things right, you know?

At the tail end of intermission, when Carl collects all the phones and pretends to "grab/steal" a few of the kids' noses like he's actually sixty, I finally text my mom back. Because that pride flag is now just sitting there a mistake, an inkblot nobody acknowledged on a nice dressy shirt.

I go with the bug-eyed, shocked emoji, and chase it with a heart.

She isn't usually fast with return texts. Not usually.

Mom takes a while to find the right emoji. It's her whole outlet; she loves her phone—it's like her secret diary or message in a bottle to an outside world that is potentially nicer than the one she chose for herself, all those years back.

My dad doesn't text.

So, normally, when I text my mom anything—"gonna be ten minutes late" or "is so you think you can dance dvr'ing?"—she takes a bit to get back to me. She marinates. Her texts are her novels, her sonnets.

She's Jankburg's own Charles Dickens—a guy who famously released his novels one chapter at a time in a newspaper, and was paid by the word. So he used a lot of words. Extra words. That's my mom, except not the extra-words part. She was a bad student, and to this day, she's always self-conscious about using the wrong word for something. She uses emojis because you can't spell an emoji wrong. She takes a while to find the right emoji and even then she usually uses only one of three.

But I text her the bug-eyed emoji and the heart today, and right away, like she's been sitting on a draft, she sends me back "<3 you back forever"

"Places for Act Two!" the stage manager yells, and a couple of the boys help Libby's mom clean up the hoagie plates, and for about eleven seconds, I don't mind being back home.

Half-Cockney, Half-Southern

At some point I should share that I'm getting a 3.0-ish GPA right now, which is not good and not bad. But it's average and I loathe being average.

Anthony—my older brother, the star athlete, and the type of kid who winks at a piece of paper and a giant A+ appears on it—never had to try that hard for good grades. But for me it's either: I'm in love with a subject (my cooking class elective) or I loathe it (most of the others).

Somebody tell me when I'm going to need algebra, when I eventually move back to New York? Like, literally, somebody, tell me.

They should teach public school children how to navigate various transportation systems across the world. Show me how to get through Paris or Chicago or Gettysburg alive, right? Or, you kids wanna move to New York? Okay, here's what you need to know about how to safely get to Queens after 11 p.m. on a weekend, when the city subway guys decide to do all their repairs.

Teach us that, adults!

I'm drawing a map of the subway system on the back of a worksheet in social studies class, desperately wishing we were studying Eva Perón (*Evita* the musical), Joseph what's-his-name (*Joseph and the Amazing Technicolor Dreamcoat*, about a blonde college student in biblical times who sings high and wears a fabulous patchwork coat), or actual Nazis (*Cabaret* and *The Sound of Music*). But we aren't. We're learning about how a bill becomes a law—and yes, I'm basically asleep.

So to stay half-awake, I'm sketching the subway by memory, the loops and turns, recalling how I'd watch rats scuttle around rooting for food. Maybe this is why I have a 3.0-ish.

But then, something happens.

Kids in my class are turning around, whispering, texting something to each other. I guess what I'm saying is: My desk is right in the middle of our social studies room, and our teacher is on the phone to the A.V. office because the Smart Board keeps short-circuiting. And some kind of rumor, or mini hurricane, is whipping around the edges of the room, working its way in, toward me. I see it happen as if I'm watching a tsunami of teen giggling occur on the horizon and gain force. It whips up strength, the text chain going off, eventually a chorus of chimes and rings and buzzes uniting in a symphony, until wham—it hits my phone too.

Ding.

Not that I haven't been bracing myself for *some* kind of news alert. It's now just a few days before our school-wide performance ($5 to get in, yes, but the cash bar was not allowed by the school board), and I've been having stomach cramps over the idea of an actor waking up with a cold, or losing a grandparent to a freak elderly person event. I was thrown on at the first preview of *E.T.* and I don't want to do it here. It wouldn't be fair, for one. I have so much more experience than the cast, and I'm a member of the actors' union, so for me to step into a role in the middle of a gym in the middle of Pennsylvania, I could be taken to Broadway jail or severely fined. Probably.

But, yeah, that's not what's going on here.

"Click on it," somebody says, gesturing to my phone.

I press the link to a video in the text—a video that has 5,800 hits, and was only uploaded last night—right as our teacher hangs up the phone, walks over to her desk, and yells, "Technology stinks! In the old days, we just had books, which don't need to be manually rebooted!"

But mostly I'm tuning her out, because mostly I'm watching my production—my *Great Expectations* that has somehow become my baby; my Nate expectations—unfold on my little phone screen.

The user who uploaded it is @BenOverBackwards_2020. Ben. My Ben. And he's good—like, a solidly decent videographer. Like, the lighting is even flattering, and it's just natural light, from Libby's backyard. From our rehearsals. That I perhaps should have kept off-camera.

This video is going viral, and it's not because people are being mean about it. It's because . . . it's great.

"Congrats, dude," says the kid behind me.

Which is when I get a funny *Did I just have bad seafood?* feeling, because I scroll down, and see that Ben has posted the time and place of my show. And that it's directed by NATE FOSTER.

In fact, the video description says:

NATE FOSTER'S
production of
CHARLES DICKENS'S
GREAT EXPECTATIONS
except . . . it's a musical!
~with songs by your parents' favorite
singers~

And then the date. And the time.

And that tickets are five bucks.

"Mr. Foster, would you like to turn your phone off and join the class?" the teacher says, but nope. No, I would not! Instead, I leap up and say, "I need to pee!" and grab my bookbag and make a run for it.

• • •

For reasons that are *insane*—I plead insanity, your dishonor—I am currently ringing the front desk of our school, tucked away in the bathroom stall upstairs, on the third floor behind the half-finished planetarium.

For further reasons of insanity, when the receptionist picks up, I slip into a sort of half-Cockney, half-Southern accent: "Hi-lo," I say, rolling my eyes at myself, "could you please call the student Ben Mendoza to the back driveway? This is his—aunt—and I need to speak with him. In person."

It's complicated to explain why I wouldn't just text him, but trust that it involves the fact that Ben is pulling a 3.9 (I know, amazing; as if he even *needed* extra credit in English), and that he feels like good grades are his way out of his own house someday. And so he walks through school all day with his phone buried in the bottom of his bag, so he won't get distracted. Kid's got discipline for days. Apparently wearing a helmet was only the tip of his responsibility iceberg. I admire it.

"His *aunt*?" the receptionist says, and I just mutter, "Mhmm," and she sighs and I think I'm a goner, will never pull this off.

But the power of my actions crackles overhead when, over our school's century-old speaker, I hear: "Could a freshman named Ben Mendoza please meet your aunt in the back driveway?"

I've already got notes for my own performance— like, I should have just told the receptionist that he's my cousin, and I have his asthma medicine; be specific so it feels less general, et cetera.

But this is how we grow as artists.

"let me guess, ur my aunt," I get as a text, one moment later, and it's from Ben, already onto me.

By the time he and I meet up, not in the back driveway but in an emergency fire-exit stairwell that Libby told me isn't actually alarmed, he's dewy and nervous and holding up his phone like it's a murder weapon in which showbiz is the victim.

"Am I in trouble?" he says.

"I mean, that's not the word I'd use. It's got almost six thousand views!"

He refreshes his phone and holds it back up. "Nate, it's up to sixteen."

"Sixteen thousand?!"

"Nate." He sits on the steps. "*Sixty* thousand."

I sit down next to him and dare myself to put my

head on his shoulder, but I chicken out, and just study the weird used gum patterns in the tile. My head's got such a mixture of feels, there needs to be a new word for it.

"Do you want me to take the video down?"

At the very moment Ben asks me that, Jordan texts me: "you didn't tell me you were using famous music and charging people for tix!" accompanied by that blank-faced emoji that can mean so many things, good or bad.

I lay my head down on my knee and for one moment pretend I'm asleep, right before the prince appears in the dream.

Genetically Wiggly Eyebrows

Adults can be helpful if you'll let them, but you have to keep a tight leash.

I'm texting Aunt Heidi, Chief Cool Adult of my life, because I feel like I've done something wrong somehow, in my show getting so much attention. Without my meaning for it to, that is. And even though Heidi doesn't always have the answer, she always has an opinion. Which is something.

"again it's v hard to explain," I'm typing to her for the twentieth time.

Finally, she just video-calls me, tired and confused by all the texting back and forth.

"First off, why aren't you in school?"

"I am." I whip my phone around. "See, I'm in the bathroom."

"Nate. Stop shaking the screen. I'm going to puke."

I lean against the handicap grab-bar and steady my phone.

"Also," Heidi says, "I've only got two minutes because I'm at a callback for an all-female production of *Hamlet* in Dallas. How can I help? Are you in some kind of trouble?"

"I don't . . . know. Technically. No? Maybe."

I feel like there's got to be some kind of manual that high school students get, that tells them how to not completely screw up their lives. And, like, I missed the manual, because I wasn't there on the first day of school.

Heidi's doing a thing where she checks for split ends like she's fifteen, which I love about her. "Just tell me what you did, Nate."

"Nothing! I mean nothing bad. I'm putting on a performance at school, and I'm using famous pop songs, and a video of the show is going . . . viral."

"Send me the link."

So I do, but it takes forever to get to her. As it's loading, Libby is texting me, "omg omg omg it's up to 75000 views this vid is liiiit."

I tell Aunt Heidi what's up and she does a very overt "gulp" sound. "That is a *lot* of views, Natey."

"Duh, I know."

"Is this a bad thing, though? My agent would kill for something I do to go viral."

"I don't know," I say. "I just have that exact funny feeling I had that one time you took me to the Indian restaurant in Queens and I ate too much none."

"Naan."

"Exactly."

The bell goes off.

"I have to go."

"Important class?"

"Lunch."

"Ah, so your favorite subject, I assume."

"First of all, how dare you; secondly: yes."

Except lunch isn't in the cards today. There will be no Mexican pizza for Bossy Nate.

Because, at that very moment, over the ancient speaker system, comes that same receptionist's voice—the one who didn't buy I was Ben's aunt, but didn't care enough to question me. "Nathan Foster," the voice says, and Heidi and I cock the same genetically wiggly eyebrow at each other over FaceTime, "to the principal's office, please."

"Nate, am I going to have to be a responsible adult right now and tell your mother that something's up?" Heidi hates when I make her be responsible.

"Don't," I say. "I think I'm about to be in official trouble somehow. I don't need you to be the warm-up act."

We hang up after saying I love you and junk, but

you don't need to know all those details.

And look, I know none of this makes sense—a viral video should be cause for celebration. But this is what real life is, when you're me, or maybe you. The minute you get good news, you wonder where the bad news is hiding.

I'm getting water, stopping at a different bathroom for a sort of unenthusiastic pee, humming and doing gentle hopscotch games all to avoid a direct route to the principal—when Libby texts me: "go look at your locker LITERALLY RIGHT NOW."

So I do.

And when I arrive, it's like . . . how do I say this. It's the way a Broadway backstage on opening night looks sort of like a funeral home—something my mom's flower shop would have furnished—except somehow even better. Because, even though at *E.T.* we got over-the-top gifts (literally massage gift certificates), everyone's dressing space looked the same. We all got the same crap. Pricey crap, but crap. I'm fourteen, I don't need a massage, I need mac and cheese and an HBO GO password.

But here! Mine is the only locker that's decorated. Balloons, glittery paper, NATE ROCKS signs. The works. It's my own mini backstage. My own funeral home, too.

"It was the stage manager's idea to decorate your

locker. There's a card," Libby says. She's behind me, I guess, and has been for a minute or so. I open it. And as I tear across the top of the yellow envelope, I realize in this second that I hope it's from Ben. That I hope he's professing a crush, or asking me to go bike riding when it isn't just to rehearsal.

But it's not.

"The whole company signed it."

It's a card from the whole *Great Expectations* cast, with little inside jokes—"I'll smile more!" from Mona Lisa; "You have reinvented lip-syncing" from our stage manager. I catch myself about to cry, emotion running up through me like a rat through a maze. Through a subway system, actually, along the tracks and running from an incoming train.

This isn't how coming home was supposed to feel. I was all prepped to be hated. My armor was up for that. I know how to struggle through the feeling of being the underdog.

I don't have enough practice at being liked.

In the corner of the card, the longest message in the best handwriting: a paragraph, from Paige, that ends with: "Not to be sappy but I've sort of met my all-time best friends doing this show and I can't believe you thought I could be a lead but I appreciate it and will forever!!! Paigey."

And right as my spit is doing its complicated

transformation process into tears (I think that's how it works, but science hasn't gotten to the bottom of this, I don't think), the voice comes on again: "Nathan Foster. Stop dawdling. You're expected in the principal's office now."

You Could Have,
but You Didn't!

I breeze past the receptionist's desk, but before I step inside the principal's office, the receptionist goes, "Your voice sure sounds a lot like Ben's aunt's," and winks at me (!).

My mouth must drop open, because the receptionist tosses me one of those ancient hard candies that old ladies keep at their desks and/or purses and/or assorted pockets, and I love her for this. "Good luck in there." I see a lipstick stain on her teeth and I weirdly want to help her. "For the record, I love the theater."

"The famous Nathan Foster!" I hear, and turn, and it's the principal, the gym coach, and Mr. English, like the set-up to a joke where there's no way I'm not the punch line.

The principal is fiddling with her computer. "How do I . . . get this thing to . . ." She's clearly watching the viral video, specifically the sequence of

Great Expectations in which Paige opens the door to her falling-down mansion. It's very *Grey Gardens*, a musical based on a true story about old women with strange accents, who sing kind of minor-key songs that work in spite of themselves.

"Nate," one of them, or all of them, say. "How does she get this to play through the speakers?"

I run around the side of the desk, and gentle-shove the principal out of the way, and say, "You've got like twenty windows open on this thing—you probably stalled it."

Mr. English pops his gum. He's a tight chewer, the type where they barely open their mouths.

"Make it stop," the principal says with a baby voice, and so I reach down and push the power button and reboot the whole system.

"Well, I could have done that," she goes.

And I can't help myself, I can't. I say, "But you didn't."

One thing my dad told me—the only really useful thing he ever said—was, "Your whole life people will tell you, well, I could have done that, once you accomplish something. And you get to look at them and say, *But you didn't*."

He said this the first time we drove to West Virginia, and Dad caught an impressive trout ("Let it live!" I shrieked), and my uncle responded to my dad:

"Well, I could've caught that." But he didn't. And the lesson applies. Whether it's a big fish or a big show, your success is going to be other people's annoyance. Dad was right about that.

"For the record, these are my favorite songs, so this is on me," Mr. English says. He's the only adult not sitting, standing instead at the window like he's the lookout for runaway convicts.

"Am I in trouble?" I say.

The coach *thwaps* his meat-hands against the arms of a chair he's too big for. "Someone wanna be responsible for telling my Paige that she can't take part in the only activity that's brought her joy since they reissued the *Mulan* DVD?"

He's growing on me like a fungus I actually enjoy. And yet: "Wait, the show is *off*?" I blurt out.

The principal, by the way, isn't even brokering the conversation. She's typing like she's trying to kill her keyboard, and then, finally, craning her neck around and shouting the receptionist's name, capping it off with: "What's my password?!"

I'm an expert at password recovery, since I was born less than twenty years ago.

"It's probably a pet, and then a series of numbers, like the last four of your social." Though it all comes out a little garbled, because the candy the receptionist gave me is so sour I'm starting to drool. Fun!

The principal sniffs twice, types quietly, and says, "Well, look at that. I'm in."

The receptionist ducks her head in and reads, off a Post-it note, "Binky-eight-five-eight-two."

"Yeah, I'm *in*," the principal says.

On the corner of her desk I see a photo of her with a very big dog, the type who rescues stranded hikers, and, engraved on the frame in a standard Microsoft cursive, BINKY FOR ALWAYS.

"Where were we?" the principal says.

I'm feeling lightheaded, and go to spit out the candy in the principal's wastebasket, but miss it entirely, and watch it skitter across the floor.

"I think someone was telling me my show is canceled even though everyone loves the music and the coach's niece is brilliant" (mild lie) "in it."

That's when the candy *ba-dangs* against a potted plant, rolls a couple times, and makes an improbable hop up onto the loafer of a man I hadn't seen until this second.

A fancy guy, in a suit, with a briefcase on his lap, seated next to a fancy woman and an even fancier smaller guy, and all of them seated in the corner of the principal's office beneath the principal's Penn State grad school certificate. Also, a pennant from our high school, that was signed by my brother after he broke the 500-meter swim record and the "free throw" gym class hoops contest, all in one week. I'll never forget it because I've done my best to block it out.

"I believe where we *were*," the first man in the loafers says after picking my candy off his shoe and wrapping it in a tissue, "was discussing our terms by which the show could go on."

While I don't know who he is, I *see* who he is. Who they all are.

Well-dressed; slick-haired; perfect dewy skin suggesting years of lavish skin ointments. Too charming, too quiet, and too unwilling to look directly at me. My father, in the only other act I now remember, warned me about people like this.

"Lawyers," I whisper.

Here's What $25,000 Will Get You in This Day and Age

So, the show is off. Like, not happening.

Let me just, uh, get that out of the way.

The lawyers all represent the musicians and "estates" (fancy word for ghosts with money), and their job is to figure out "where in the world people are using our songs without permission," and then "go shut them down. Or get them to pay up."

What a cool job, I'll add sarcastically.

"But it was just going to be in a gym!" I say, and the coach says, "A great gym, one of the best gyms in the state," but the female lawyer isn't having it, and neither is the small guy or the tall guy.

We all share a nice, big, throat-opening laugh over the amount of money they each want—"Twenty-five thousand dollars to use any of our clients' songs in a performance for which you're charging money."

Which, I learn in front of these adults, is more

than "the entire budget for the school's anti-drug program *plus* the after-school activities program *plus* the parking lot repavement efforts—for an entire year!" This, from the principal, who knocks over her beloved Binky photo, flailing her arms around.

But "Twenty-five grand is the figure," the lawyers keep saying, and nobody's budging.

We watch them exit to the only nice cars in the parking lot—two BMWs and an actual Porsche in a sea of Kias. They're all midnight black and shiny and look like no bug has ever died in its path. Only shows. Only shows and dreams die in the path of a lawyer.

"I hate lawyers," the principal says, and we all scatter away without saying much, heads hung low, the coach looking more disappointed than even I feel. But maybe I'm just numb.

"What if we just didn't charge the audience?" Libby says later, when we climb out onto the roof of the "bonus" classrooms out on the north side of the lawn, where a bunch of mobile home classrooms went up last spring after the school board discovered asbestos in the main building. I'm picking up little pieces of slate from the roof, and flicking them off, and listening for them to land, but they don't make a sound.

"Yeah, I tried that idea, but the first lawyer said now that the show had been announced—thanks to

Ben's video—we either pay their fee, or they yank the rights to all the songs."

Libby is taking it worse than I am, in a way. I've gone numb, like when I found out Feather had a gall bladder infection, or that my dad and mom were going through a rocky time. I never cry at the normal stuff. I cry if *So You Think You Can Dance* doesn't record on the DVR, or if a boy I shared my first kiss with has gone weird on me. But even then, I don't cry instantly. It wells up, pools under my skin, creates a clot. And then I'll, like, spill potato chips all over the kitchen floor, and the clot will break open and I'll cry over Ruffles, but not real life.

"I *knew* we should have told Ben to yank the video," Libby says, and I cluck and go, "Girl, you were so excited to have those hits, you were feeling yourself," and she pushes me and says, "Shut up," but doesn't mean it. Because I'm right.

"So, what do we do?" I say, brushing my hands together and seeing them glow like I'm the tin man, shiny with silver slate powder from the roof.

"You tell *me*, director," she says, and takes a pen to autograph her shoe across the toe. It looks great. She's trying out a new thing where none of the letters are capitalized, a lowercase *l* leading into an *i*. I wish we could get graded on the journey our autographs have taken over the years. I'd pull a 4.0 no matter what.

Signs

The coach—*distraught* is not too strong a word—graciously allows me to use the gym for our final run-through tonight.

Mom's stuck at the shop and Dad's off early from work, so he drives me wordlessly over to rehearsal, says he might stick around and wait for me, maybe run some laps on the old track behind the old auditorium. See if he's "still got it," as if I'm going to find sports-talk fun, or bonding.

I say, "Cool," and head into the gym early. Couldn't eat dinner beforehand. That kind of night.

The cast appears in one big clump of kids, all at once. I hear them before I see them, parading down the halls after dark, the only fun time to be at school.

At first, weeks ago, people came to my rehearsals as individuals, heads down, phones out. But they're a family now. They arrive together, limbs intertwined, inside jokes ringing out like songbirds in the morning.

But it isn't the morning. It's the Thursday night before we're supposed to put on the show, right here in the gym, and I have to crush them all with the news.

I wait till everyone has found a place on the bleachers, and the role reversal of it all hits me. What I mean is: I've never stood in any gym and been the one in charge.

I've stood and been chosen last.

I've been pummeled with dodgeballs, and humiliated on shirts-and-skins day.

I've practiced balance beam on the basketball court outline, back before I knew not to. And pretended the rope climb was a final audition for *Tarzan* (overrated movie, underrated musical, still playing in Germany!).

But in those moments, those early years—and hours that felt like years—it was always a countdown. If I can just get through the next forty minutes, I'd chant like a mantra, I'll be okay. Thirty-nine minutes more. Twenty minutes more. Five minutes more and I can get a sip of water and get out of here.

And now I don't want this moment to be over. Or start, really.

"Is he going to say something?" I hear one of the girls say, and I'm on.

But just when I open my mouth to say, "Listen up,

guys, I've got some crappy news," Ben leaps up. He's in the front row of the bleachers, of course. Ben is a kid who doesn't mind sitting in the front and looking eager.

He wants a ticket out of this place and he knows that life is first-come, first-served.

"Hold up, Foster," he says. "Before you say anything."

He steps over a stray bookbag, is standing ten feet away from me.

This is probably where Ben's going to thank me for introducing him to theater. And then, I dunno, intro his *girlfriend*, and in a surprise twist, point to Paige. That's the way my life usually goes. Building to a moment and then pulling it out from beneath me.

But just as I'm bracing for Ben's big reveal, that he's actually hopelessly in love with a girl and grateful I got him out of the house, instead he nods his head at Jim-Jim, who lifts up his phone and begins playing Carly Rae Jepsen's seminal hit, "Call Me Maybe," which will be dated faster than milk but goes down pretty easy right now.

Ben starts wiggling around.

Now, he is a terrible dancer, a terrible mover even, frequently getting his pants legs caught in his bike spokes on the way to rehearsal. Tonight, he's tripping over his feet, trying to re-create a weaving pattern we picked up from the opening number of *A Chorus Line* that I made him watch on YouTube a couple weeks ago.

He's terrible. It's . . . everything.

He's lip-syncing the lyrics to "Call Me Maybe," and I have no idea what is going on, except that Libby is filming the entire thing on her phone, and I think maybe I'm going to throw up, except I didn't have anything for dinner.

When he gets to the lyric about how, before I came into his life, he missed me "so bad" (insane lyric with grammar all over the place), the cast begins standing. One row at a time. From the back to the front. Like cheerful, cheerleading robots.

And at this point I'm not worried I'm going to throw up so much as that they're all about to do something to humiliate me.

"Nate!" Ben whisper-shouts above the music. "Read the signs."

And that's when I realize they are each holding a large piece of poster board, big handmade signs. And that one by one, starting with Jim-Jim, and then on to Mona Lisa, and on and on and on, they start flipping the signs around to spell something out.

For me.

Ben is still dancing. I'm telling you, he's adorably horrible and totally off the beat.

I squint at the signs. I've never been good at word games. Please, don't let this be hard to solve:

An *H*, and then an *E*, and a *Y* get flipped around.

"Hey," I say out loud, to myself.

And then an *I* sign, and a *J*, and more and more and faster and faster, flipping like a perfect card trick—*U, S, T.*

"Hey," "I," "Just," I'm memorizing like a locker combo to a new school where you're actually doing pretty okay.

They're spelling the lyrics to this ridiculous candy bop of a song.

That's when I see a bunch of parents gathered at the door of the gym, all of them watching this not-at-all-spontaneous act—this must have taken a week to coordinate.

I sit down cross-legged on the gym floor, 'cause I don't have anything to hold on to. And Ben laughs.

A *Y* sign, an *O*, a senior whose name is either Jackie or Jacklyn, who can remember, holding a particularly sparkly *U* (extra points to her, you can tell she used up a lot of glue). And then three kids mix up the spelling of *A-N-D*, their signs in the wrong order, and I yell, "I got it, you're spelling *and*," and Ben shushes me.

That's when I see my dad, wandering in from the old racetrack, to spy on the commotion. It's like

Where's Waldo? except he's not in stripes, and I find him right away.

He's just standing there in the doorway to the gym with the rest of the parents, and he's dead-faced, or maybe I mean Dad-faced. Neutral. Which is, to be fair, sometimes my particular dad's version of an endorsement.

If he tolerates something, that's as good as go.

"Keep reading!" I hear someone say, and I flip my head back, and try to catch up, but the letters get scrambled. I'm thinking it's amazing and probably will someday seem like a beautiful irony that Ben has struggled with dyslexia his whole life, and he's choosing to spell out some big announcement to me.

This isn't how I was planning on coming out. I was hoping I'd be an international Broadway celebrity, established in my career back in New York by age twenty, maybe twenty-three tops. And I'd have some really cool boyfriend. And I'd intro my parents to him over FaceTime from a party at the top of the Empire State Building, and if it got awkward, I'd say "Reception sucks!" and hang up. And kiss him.

But it appears I don't get to direct this particular scene.

The signs keep folding out, one after another, and it strikes me that this must have been what it felt like to read *Great Expectations*, back in the day. You think it's going one way and then boom, it doesn't—Dickens surprises you, takes you on a twist, leaves you wanting to read more in next week's edition of the paper, in spite of how annoying the wait is.

That's when I see my name spelled out, *N-A-T-E*, and then

W-I-L-L and *Y-O-U* and *G-O* and *T-O*—

And this—right here—is when Ben asks me to Homecoming in front of the entire cast, all of their parents, and my *D-A-D*, dad.

The song cuts out at the most awkward time—right when they're trying to spell *W-I-T-H* and *M-E* in time to the final pumping drumbeat.

Somebody throws Ben one last oversize piece of cardboard—a used Best Buy box, something a dad's TV might come.

I pinball-wizard my eyes to my own dad, who is now as red as Mars—and that makes me think about how I made my Broadway debut in a show about aliens, and how just-right that is. Because I feel like an alien myself sometimes.

Almost all the time, really.

Does that ever happen to you?

"Well?" Ben says, and I look back to see that he's holding a question mark sign, a big hand-drawn question mark that was colored in with a green marker that lost its ink halfway through. I feel my own color draining, my white-hot white face.

Green is my favorite color, which I didn't know he knew. But Ben just seems to be able to predict me.

"Say something!" Libby yells, and Jackie or Jacklyn goes, "Wooo."

And even though my head is full of prepared remarks—and the image of my red dad, and the echoey gym sound that makes me think of all the times I sat in this very auditorium and watched my brother beat some state sports record—I attempt to go off-script. To answer Ben with: "This is extremely flattering, let's . . . talk about this one-on-one!"

But I don't. I can't.

Because, "The show is canceled, guys," I hear, before I can talk. "Nate's trying to tell us the show is canceled." It's Paige who's saying it. The coach must have pre-broken the news to her, before tonight's big meeting.

Somebody laughs, and then somebody shushes them. Because they can probably tell that I'm as red and as real and in some ways as far away as Mars too.

Warning Labels

M_y older brother, Anthony, once shared something wise and insightful—which is really something,
because usually when he's talking to me, it's to tell me
to shut up.

Anyway, he once said that the only way he and my
dad could connect is if "one of their other senses was
being occupied at the same time." Like, playing catch
out back, or even just driving somewhere. Anywhere.
They could talk only when they weren't looking at
each other.

But I don't want to test the concept.

So afterward—after the great Homecoming
debacle—I tell my dad I'm just going to bike home,
and he nods, doesn't say anything.

We pretend it didn't even happen.

He has always been so big to me—tall, yeah, but
also just big as a concept. And so, to have seen him,

the last of the parents, sitting on the benches, the same benches he used to sit on, back when he played basketball for this same high school; and to see him in his bad-fitting dad jeans and a red baseball hat? It's hard to notice how small he seems to me now. Even though, I guess it makes us something closer to equals.

"Can I ride with you?" Libby says, even though she doesn't have a bike. And I say, "Of course," and my dad lets us be.

I walk my bike home and she walks beside me and mostly she checks her texts and we don't say much.

But at some point, I stop walking my bike, and pull out my phone, and text Ben: "for the record that was crazy sweet of you to organize that homecoming thing, and I was very tongue tied, and didn't have anything to eat before rehearsal. so I'm sorry if I was completely weird, and in director mode."

Send. Breathe. Walk.

Twenty minutes later Libby and I are in the old treehouse that my dad built me, back when he thought I'd take after Anthony, and enjoy playing things like robbers and cowboys and tree ninjas. Instead I used the tree fort as a place to practice my one-man *Robin Hood* musical, to the acclaim of over twelve wild chipmunks.

Somehow it's easier to talk up here, because I feel like a kid again. And when you're a kid, you still have so many chances to get your life right.

"I bet this thing is infested with like a thousand termites now," Libby says, rather unhelpfully, when we're sitting knee-to-knee, crisscross applesauce, on our old treehouse lookout tower.

"I should have grabbed Capri Suns from the fridge in the garage," I say. I can tell we're both thirsty. You can just tell these things about your best friend.

She scrolls her phone mindlessly. "That's okay, I can't stay long. Mom and I are supposed to be watching a documentary tonight."

"You watch documentaries now?" I say. I can hear how tired my voice is. It takes a lot of yelling to quiet down a freaked-out cast—one that wants to put on the show no matter what. You should have seen the way they started drooping their big, glittery, lettered poster board signs, one after another, in shock, and losing all sense of control.

"On Thursdays, yeah. Thursdays are documentary nights now. You know my ma." I do. She's the greatest lady. She makes plans for Libby. Most moms are good at either coming up with cool ideas or following through with them, but Libby's mom is good at both.

I'm just starting to say, finally, at last, "I can't believe that boy asked me to Homecoming," when Libby holds up her phone and says, "Wanna watch the video?"

"Duh."

Generally I hate how I look-slash-sound in any video, but . . . I don't know. I think I'm growing into my body a little? Like, not to be cocky. Just a fact. I used to be a full-on pear-shaped boy. But now I'm more like an orange or something.

I dart my tongue over my lips. I could use a drink, and some dinner, too. It's been over four hours since a real meal, and the bark on the tree that rams through the base of this fort is starting to look like artisanal chocolate.

"So, you were in on it the whole time?" I ask.

"On what?"

"The, like, proposal." Even saying the word *proposal* makes me go Mars-red.

"I was. So were some of the parents."

"Some of them," I repeat back.

Libby mischief-grins and pockets her phone. "But if you want the deets, you should ask *him*."

She chin-points toward my house, where Ben himself is lurking behind a bush, mouthing something like he's practicing a line, and reaching to knock on the window of the darkened bedroom I'm not even in.

"What a creeper," I say through a smile.

Libby clears her throat extra loud and swings her legs down over the side of the fort, and Ben turns around like we're a couple of stars of a vampire musical (vampires in musicals never work—there is a graveyard full of flops to prove me right).

I see him nearly drop a big Tupperware container.

"Hey," I say, and he goes, "Hey," and Libby says, "And here's my exit," and is gone around the side of the house in three seconds flat.

"You're . . . here!"

"Is that okay?"

I don't know what to say, truly. "You are so good in the show and I'm sorry it's canceled."

"Am I, though?" he says, and kicks some driveway gravel into our sorry excuse for grass. Libby's back-yard is green like the question-mark sign Ben held for me. Our grass is brown as a bad cloud.

"You are good! Yeah, you totally are. You've come a long way in the acting department."

Awkward pause. Awkward pause. We could really use a big lighting-cue change or orchestral under-scoring here. Musicals are so much easier than life, and musicals are *hard*.

He holds out the Tupperware, which makes me realize how close I'm standing to him. "Oh, I brought you something."

"Me?"

I take it, and it's hot, and I'm burning my ten-der, non-calloused fingers, just as he's saying, "It's probably still pretty warm," and I lie and say, "Nah, it's totes fine," even though I want to scream. About everything.

I lift the lid and the steam makes my eyes go watery.

"Yeah, sooo. There's a lot of vinegar in that. Maybe too much."

He looks worried, so I blurt, "I love vinegar!" as if that's a thing, but he goes, "Cool," so I guess it's cool.

"Is it . . . chicken?"

"Yeah, leftover-but-still-amazing chicken adobo. Traditional Filipino dish. Grandma's recipe."

It smells amazing once you stop coughing.

"Did your mom make it or something?"

"Ha!" He grumble-laughs too hard and then goes, "Nah, she doesn't cook much. I cook for us. We had extra because she's never hungry."

"And you thought I'd want some?" I say. And as if I'm attending the musical of my own life story, I watch as the unlikely star (me) grabs a piece of chicken and takes a bite. And it's unreal. It's a flavor party and I'm the only guest.

The unlikely star is grinning like an idiot who's never had a good meal in his life.

"I figured you're probably bummed out about the show," Ben says as I navigate around a tricky bay leaf. "I'm always hungry when I'm bummed out."

"That's funny, my mom always loses her appetite when she's upset. I think she hasn't had anything to eat in thirty years."

He laughs again.

"But you didn't answer my question," he says with no warning. This is a kid who could really use a warning label. "About Homecoming."

Ding-a-ling. That's when Jordan's FaceTime comes in, followed by an urgent text: "HELP! Need your advice to choose between two new headshots!!! <3"

I hit Ignore, and look up, and catch a shadow—my mom moving away from a curtain that's half-broken in our living room, hanging from a single loop around a rod that we've got to get replaced.

And in this moment I don't want Ben to see the way my house is never quite clean—but then I remember that he's got it worse. That he found me. That it was my window he knocked on.

Like a dumbo, I say, "Yeah, about Homecoming: If I don't have anything going on that night, sure."

Ben eyeroll-laughs, but this time it's like a howl. I try to pivot from the weirdness, and from the fact that I oddly feel like I need my parents' permission to go to Homecoming—but how am I ever going to begin that conversation? Sure, Dad watched the proposal happen—heck, he showed *up* for it—but if I never mention it again, we can pretend it didn't happen.

I wanted to come out on the roof of the Empire State Building.

No—I wanted my insides to feel more sure of themselves before I announced my outsides. It's that. That's the problem here.

I wanted to feel ready.

And so to keep the scene moving, I say, "I'll bring you back the Tupperware when I'm done. And, like, I'll clean it and stuff."

He waves it off. "Don't bother." And gets back on his bike, no helmet this time. "My mom never notices when stuff is missing."

He pedals away, way faster than normal. And I kick the rocks from our grass back onto the gravel. And then I sit down against the vinyl siding of our house, and finish the entire chicken dish, all the leftovers, stopping just short of licking the Tupperware.

But at the end, I still feel hungry.

Thriller Night

It's the morning of the show, but there's no show to put on.

Nothing is sadder than a clown without a balloon or a magician without a dove.

Mr. English keeps me after class. "I'm very upset for you," he says. "I was looking forward to hearing those songs and I'm sure it's a big disappointment."

I'm about to ask him if that means I automatically get an A. That'd be nice.

But he says, "You're going to have to figure out a way to bring your grade up, though, Nate. So far you've gotten a bunch of Cs on my quizzes. I can tell you aren't doing even the in-class assignments, and that you've got your head somewhere else."

I unzip my bookbag, but I can't find any gum. "So, I don't get credit for all the weeks I put into the show?"

"I can give partial credit. Because, of course. I can

always grade that iPhone video of the rehearsal. But even if the show had gone on, you've treated this project like it's your entire grade, Mr. Foster. It isn't. You're behind on tests, on in-class assignments . . . it's not good."

He gets a text and he answers it, right in front of me.

"Is there something else you need?" he asks after I stand there just looking at him for a while.

"I mean, I guess not?"

Libby's waiting by the door, and I walk out feeling like I'm a billion pounds of leftovers. Mr. English asks me to close the door behind me on the way out, and Libby walks me to math, a.k.a. the seventh circle of doom.

When I finally look up to say goodbye to Libby and tell her I'll see her at lunch, that's when I see her *I've got an idea* face. And that's when Libby tells me her idea. "Something for the dorks" is how she puts it, and I'm sold.

• • •

You can barely fit all the parents in Libby's backyard— and this is a family with a big backyard. They've got one of those little sheds where dads store hoses and junk, and patio stones that aren't broken. And furniture. And enough space for two kids to grow up a little wild. It's nice. And now it's full of parents.

The coach arrives, and it's so odd to see him in

non-gym clothes that I literally don't recognize him at first. He's got flowers for Paige and it's just super sweet and pure.

"I'm going to tell the stage manager to tell the cast it's twenty minutes till showtime," Libby says, pulling me away from the gathering crowd in her foyer.

She's got the kind of family who's got a foyer.

"Just wait till fifteen minutes," I say, impatient and feeling like a hot tub with the jets set to blast mode. "*That's* when stage managers call. Not twenty. It's half hour, then fifteen, then ten, then five, then places."

"Nate?" Libby says, pinching my cheek like she's some kind of elderly relative. "You aren't on Broadway anymore, and if we want to tell the cast it's *seventeen* minutes till showtime, we can. My house, my rules!"

She winks, and runs upstairs two steps at a time, past all her framed class photos and one poster we hand-made from a production of *Godspell* we put on—just her and me, in her backyard. A production that we set in the Depression, because *Godspell* is very flexible that way. Very cool concept. Jesus was a millionaire. It worked.

You know what's not working, though? The fact that Ben isn't here. As in, one of my actors isn't in the building. And I have his Tupperware all cleaned out and everything.

I've been trying not to worry about his being late, but I can't not—I'm more upset that *he's* not here than that my mom is working overtime at the shop tonight, prepping flowers for a surprise funeral. And my dad is at the hospital, pulling a double maintenance shift to cover for a buddy of his who's fishing.

I half thought of bringing Feather along, just to have a friendly face in the audience. But I was afraid she'd pee all over our set.

Libby texts me: "the girls are all freaking out upstairs that they've run out of hairspray because girls are the worst" and then "maybe u should give a speech to the audience before the show?"

It's all too much, really—I'm all about outdoor theater, when it wants to be outdoors. But I'd kind of fallen in love with the gym concept. Once the principal forbade us from using it, however—apparently it would be some kind of "school board liability," now that lawyers were involved—we had no other choice.

When we call places, Ben still isn't here, so I text the stage manager "should we stall????" Even though Ben doesn't make his first entrance for forty minutes. It doesn't matter. I want to die and faint and disappear, and rewind everything.

And never let Jordan be my first kiss.

That's when I hear, "Oh gosh, you didn't start, did you?"

I turn around and of course it's Ben, and standing next to him—my dad (!) and mom (?).

If three ghosts had walked in on stilts, I'd probably be less shocked.

"We should probably get the kid some ice," my dad says, and that's when I notice Ben's torn jeans, his bloody knee, gravel burnt in his palms.

"Had a little bike mishap," he says, sweaty bangs plastered to his forehead. "But luckily, your parents drove by, and stopped, and picked me up in their car."

"We were going to come surprise you," Mom says. "We both took the night off." She puts her hand on Ben's shoulder. "I'm just sorry the backseat was full of so much junk."

"Ben!" the stage manager calls from the top of Libby's stairs. "You're here!"

The stage manager hurries down, way too zippy, and right when she's at the bottom, I want to yell, "Slow down, because the second-to-the-last step is unevenly spaced and I've been falling off it for a decade," but I don't have time to. And she wipes out (but recovers nicely).

"That's my name," he says, "Ben," looking a little disoriented.

But, like, so adorable too.

Libby's mom pulls Ben into the kitchen, and all at once the rest of the audience makes their way out back and finds about twenty odd chairs. But mostly they just stand like they're guests at a weird party thrown by kids.

Which makes me the host.

It's still light out, no proper time for a musical, but that's what's funny about theater. The show must go on.

Now, this is the moment when Ben's mom shows up, right? Right?

We've been talking about her, hinting about her, all her troubles and how she is never there for Ben, even when he cooks up traditional chicken dishes and bikes over to the market, point-seven miles away, to grab her sodas after 10 p.m. on a school night.

It would be a great moment for a Mom Mendoza entrance. But she doesn't show up. Because even though musicals usually end with a big production number, life isn't like that.

And so, this is the moment—as Libby pushes me out onto the patch of grass we're calling our stage— that Mr. English arrives, right? *Right?*

Like, he's decided to give up one of his nights, maybe. He always says that "from 2:30 p.m. till 7 a.m. the next morning," his time is "*all* his," which is why old Mr. English famously doesn't give a lot of homework but *does* give the toughest tests in the school. But maybe not tonight. Maybe tonight Mr. English shows up, for me: a student he secretly adores for his grit and wit, right?

Nah, you've seen too many movies and maybe a few plays, too.

Mr. English doesn't show up. And neither does Ben's mom.

But when I cough a couple times and tell myself to stand up straight like a tree (good technique for not looking nervous: imitate something stationary), and then welcome the audience to our show, I see my dad put his hand on my mom's shoulder.

A first in forever.

And neither of them looks at their phones, or away from me, I guess. Like, I guess that's the bigger deal.

"Enjoy yourselves, if you can!" I say, and then "Please be forgiving, because we don't have the best sound system out here."

Libby's mom yells "*Hey!*" 'cause it's her house and everything and parents are obsessed with looking "faux-offended but in a fun way" in front of one another.

And that's it. There's nothing more to say. We're not doing this for a grade, we're doing this for us.

I exit the patch of grass we're calling our stage, and run smack-dab right into Ben ~wham~ who is, of course, filming everything. And who says "Ow" in a sweet way.

And whose breath smells like peppermint and nerves.

He bites down hard on a mint and squeezes my hand, and he inhales as if to say, "So, Homecoming, yes, no?"

But I don't let him get a word out or a question in. I get professional, and pat him on the shoulder, and I say, "Have a great show."

And then I can't help it—I look back out to the audience, and see my dad seeing me. And I wonder if he told my mom about last night, at the gym. About the red-faced proposal. If my parents went to bed together for the first time in ages and if Dad confessed that he saw another boy ask me to a dance.

A bug lands on my shoulder and I look at it and wonder if the bugs will bite my actors in this weirdly humid autumn night, or if anyone is going to forget their lines, or if my parents even know how much it means that they gave up some extra work shifts to be here for me.

Jim-Jim must have pressed Play, because the howling cemetery music starts. Then we cut to Michael Jackson's "Thriller" (it's a great moment, and gets a big parent-roar). And then the stage manager runs around, placing graveyards all over the grass. And I actually wish I'd brought Feather now. She'd be so proud of me.

Maybe next time.

Boys Are Overrated

We have a cast party that turns into a crew party that ends up on Libby's roof watching shooting stars.

Ben doesn't stick around—he has to go "check on his mom." But we get a good solid hug in, in Libby's foyer, and I give him back his Tupperware, and he swears his knee will be fine and that I'm lucky I have the type of parents who'd stop to help a kid on the side of the road. And he just leaves, like that. No big goodbye.

He leaves and I stay, because it's my party and I'll stay if I want to? I'm doubting myself, though.

But all is not lost, or not awkward, at least. Several of the parents called my musical "*the* best show" they'd ever seen, and one of them even has a subscription to the Pittsburgh Public Theater (which puts on legit shows like Shakespeare), so I took it as a huge compliment. I'm *taking* it as a huge compliment.

And Paige was outrageous, by the way. Meryl Streep in braces. She nailed it.

She was hired as a favor—okay, "cast" as a favor, since nobody got paid anything—and it turns out she embodied Miss Havisham like nobody could have imagined. She seemed so old and haggard and past her prime that if it weren't for the fact that she sweat off most of the grey powder in her hair, I think people really would have thought we'd hired an old lady as a guest artist.

The gym coach cried.

And apparently he told Libby's mom that he's working on a "top secret, don't-tell-anyone plan to get an arts program going again at the school," and that he's even gonna volunteer his gym as the auditorium.

How cool is that. Don't tell anyone, though, because it's top secret, ha-ha.

Now, the less said about Pip the better, I suppose. True, he didn't forget any of his lines. And when he stepped right through a cardboard headstone in the first scene, and a few of the dads chuckled, he bravely pretended like it didn't happen. Even as he dragged that dang headstone around by a shoelace for the rest of the scene.

His parents led the standing ovation. And yes, for a full picture: They were already standing, leaning against the fence for the whole show. But some of the parents got to sit, and by the end they were all on their feet, whistling.

Jim-Jim and Mona Lisa were excellent. Good enough to understudy their roles, if we'd actually done this thing professionally.

Which, let's be honest—we never will.

"Am I fooling myself that it was pretty great?" I say to Libby, about twenty minutes after one of the kids half pukes off the side of her roof, due to an over-abundance of pizza and Mountain Dew.

"Nah, they killed it," Libby says.

She checks in on the puking kid and then kicks him off her roof, through the window that leads to the attic that we haven't played in for forever.

"I'm sort of glad so many of the parents were video-ing it," I say, leaning back and now sharing a small bowl of candy corn with Libby. She's always got Halloween candy around, no matter the season. "I wanna send it to Mr. English and be like: *See?* You should have given up a night for this."

"I think he just knows you're super smart and is giving you a hard time."

"That's like the lamest line that adults say," I say. "That they're hardest on the kids they see the most potential in. Bull."

Libby whimpers, and swear-shouts: "*Tuck Everlasting!*" (sixty-seven performances on Broadway, lovely folksy score, based on a book about people who never die, which sounds exhausting), and then turns to me and says, "I think a rogue candy corn just chipped my front tooth."

"Show me."

She does an over-the-top fang smile.

"Perfect. You're golden. Pretty as ever."

She snort-laughs, picks a nail, and waves goodbye to a couple of sophomores whose moms are honking in the driveway below.

"Yeah, well, tell that to the boys. That I'm pretty as ever."

"What boys?"

"All boys."

"Boys are overrated," I say, "and not worth the drama."

"Ha, okay."

I sit up on an elbow. "What's that supposed to mean—*ha, okay.*"

"It means, 'a' of all, you *are* a boy, and 'b' of all, you don't seem to have trouble in the crush department."

I sit back and try to count stars.

"Jordan is really full of himself, but in a weird way I feel like if he had somehow hologrammed himself here tonight to cheer me on, I would have felt, like, so honored and dizzy. He still makes me so, like, generally confused."

"Well, to quote you, boys are overrated and not worth the drama."

I squint at a night cloud. This will sound cosmic and dumb, but I swear to you it's got the exact outline of Ben's profile.

"Does that not look like Ben's soliloquy?" I say, shaking Libby's shoulder and pointing at the sky.

"What do you mean, *soliloquy*?"

"Like, his, like, sideways profile-thing. There, his nose. There, his funny lip with the little scar. And there, his spiky hair that always looks messy."

"Buster, you mean *silhouette*."

Oh. Right. "I really have to start paying more attention in English," I say, and we bust a gut so hard that it's like the old days.

"Do you think we'll keep in touch in college?" Libby asks.

"Uh, let's just get through high school first," I say.

I take another handful of candy corn, despite my belly starting to hurt, and throw them down the hatch. And I'm about to say to Libby, "Do you think I should go to Homecoming with Ben?" when her mom texts her.

She holds up the phone for me to read: "Natey's parents called and they think he should ride his bike home now before it gets too late ☹"

So, that's it, then. A one-night-only show, and the night's over.

"You had your signature *about-to-ask-Libby-advice* face on, back there," Libby says after I've strapped on my helmet and said my last goodbyes, and am standing out there on the lawn feeling like we should be celebrating till 4 a.m. and not just till 10:30 p.m.

"It's nothing," I say, because I've already made up my mind about the dance.

And what I've decided is: If I get home, and Ben is

- outside my room, or
- texts me one more time, or
- any other sign that is clearly a sign,

I will say yes.

I start to pedal away, but I turn back around, and: "Hey, Lib."

She's leaning on their mailbox, like it's a porch. "Yeah, captain."

"Of course we'll keep in touch in college—because I plan on being your roommate."

She laughs. "You're so cray. They don't let boys and girls room together."

I spin the wheels on my bike with my foot, but I don't go anywhere. "Lib," I say, pointing toward her backyard. "After that, tonight, we aren't just a boy and a girl."

"What are we, then?"

"*Legends.*"

She taps her hand on the mailbox. "Or something."

"Yeah." Or something.

The Ben cloud overhead dissipates into a billion water particles, and it rains on my whole ride home. I can't decide if it's a sign, or if it's just weather.

Christmas Except Not

I take the longest post-show shower ever and I even wash behind my ears and stuff, though I'll spare you the details.

But after I get out and towel off and *gently* check the window: no Ben in sight.

No texts on my phone.

No follow-up. No sign.

The cloud wasn't him and it *was* just weather.

"Knock-knock." Great. It's my dad.

"One sec."

"No rush."

I slip on my old pj pants and an *E.T.* T-shirt and meet him in the hall, because one of the very coolest things about my dad is that he'll say *knock-knock* but never actually come in. Probably because of what he's afraid he'd find in my room: a stray wig, a karaoke machine, et cetera. This room is *not* his brand.

"Come on," he mumble-says, and leads me down the hall, past Anthony's room, with the Nerf hoop on the outside that not even once have I tried to "make" or "score on."

And then, past our one family bathroom that I got so foggy, he'll probably yell at me for leaving my towel on the floor.

But he doesn't.

And then, around the corner to just outside the basement door. He makes a *shh* sign, and I'm doing a tally: The only other time Dad has ever pulled me aside for a guy-talk was when Mom had health problems a couple years ago, and he had to break it to me that she was going into the hospital overnight for her heart to be looked at, but that it would probably all be okay because the health care was top-notch in Pittsburgh.

"Am I in trouble?" I say, but he doesn't answer. He just turns Mars-red again, and leads me downstairs, to our perma-damp storage closet, where we keep the Christmas lights. And now I'm really confused, because we haven't taken out the Christmas lights in ages. They're a tangle-palooza.

And it's not Christmas.

"Look, if this is about the fact that I borrowed one of Grandma's old dresses for the musical tonight, I can get it dry-cleaned."

231

He rolls his eyes, opens the storage room door, and says, "Jump on the step stool, because I'll hurt my back if I try to pull down that big Tupperware."

Suddenly my life is all Tupperware, a mystery wrapped in microwaveable plastic.

He points above, and the container says "Dad's Old Junk" in magic marker.

And I'll exactly die if he's attempting to give me a tool belt or a knife set to turn me normal.

Maybe he hated the show? And a tool belt or a knife set is his way of saying, *Let's not forget you're still my son.*

But that's not what happens.

I get on the step stool, and pull Dad's Old Junk box off the shelf, but it doesn't jangle like tools would. Dad grabs my shoulder because I fall back, thinking the box would be heavier with Guy Stuff. And when I'm back down on the safe cement floor, I'm so lost I could use a GPS, or a clue.

"What are you, about five foot five these days?" he mumble-says, and I squinch up my face and say, "My résumé says five three, since I'm still trying to play young. But yeah, technically, I'm about five five–ish."

"Good." He cracks open the top of the container and it's got closet breath, old and mothy, but he waves it off and pulls out a big ash-grey clump of fabric.

"What's this?"

He shakes it out, unrolls it, revealing a suit. A

man's suit. And he holds it up to me and it's one of those moments where you can tell it'll fit perfectly.

"Go show your mother. Get her opinion on if it looks too old-fashioned or if it'll work."

"For what? Dad, you're totally confusing me."

He shuts the closet door and clicks his tongue, the thing he does when he's nervous.

"For *Homecoming*, you little doofus."

He clicks his tongue again and tries a smile that gets all caught up in his mustache.

For the *Homecoming dance*, if you missed that.

"Are you . . . sure?"

Is he sure about lending me the suit, I guess I'm asking, but also: Wait, you're sure about *me*?

Somehow I end up hugging him. If I pull away, he'll see my face, all out of order, a Rubik's Cube before solving. So I keep hugging him.

"Yeah," he says, and he's the one who pulls away, but only barely.

He hits the lights, which is always our cue to go upstairs. "That Ben kid was good in your little play."

Musical, I don't say, because I can't say anything right now.

"If you're going to go to Homecoming, might as well go with someone as talented as you."

News flash—listen, up, important, here: If you stop believing in your parents long enough, it turns out they can occasionally come around and rock your entire world.

At the top of the stairs, right before opening the door to show off the suit for Mom, I say, "You know what, Dad, you're alright," and he just clicks his tongue again, and his voice cracks, and he says, "Well, are you going to try on the suit or not, you little doof."

And it does. Fit perfectly. By the way.

When Mom sees me in the suit, she cries. "You look like your dad when he took *me* to Homecoming!"

They met so young, you wouldn't believe it.

So I cry too—sure, why not, it's been a big day. And my dad doesn't exactly cry, but he does pet Feather in a way that's so aggressive it's like he's sending his mixed emotion–rays into the dog via its fur. But Feather's into it, and shakes her leg a bunch.

So two of us are crying and one of us is clicking his tongue and Feather is in heaven. Which is sometimes as good as real life gets.

When I'm barely falling asleep about an hour later, I realize something kind of big.

What I realize is that *I* am the sign.

That it's not on Ben to give my story a good ending. That it's on me.

"did u get home okay?" I text him.

And he texts right back: "yeah, got caught in some rain but it felt good."

I take a look at the grey suit, hanging on the handle of my closet. I can't believe my dad was ever as short as me. No, wait—I can't believe I was ever as tall as him.

"by the way, mendoza......of course I'll go to homecoming with you...if you'll still have me????" I type, and hit Send, and hold my breath so hard that I might pass out.

"akjdsflasjglkjasadf;asljdalklkgj," Ben texts right back, and then: "Phew! Yes! Yay!!!!"

And when I lick my smiling lips, it's like for two seconds I can still taste the chicken adobo on them. But not in a gross way. Sometimes the savory stuff is the sweetest stuff, too.

Airplane Mode

I'm in the midst of this amazing awake-dream where I'm literally *inside* the pages of one of Aunt Heidi's self-help books. The ones she keeps by the toilet back in New York, next to a "Harmony"-scented candle.

Anyway, moving home has made me a big softie, because here I am, half-conscious, balled up in bed, feeling like I'm skip-dancing from page to page inside this big ol' Nate-size advice book. Picture a medically small boy jumping from inspirational quote to inspirational quote, most of them involving "breathing deep" and "honoring the moment." Swinging from letter to letter, like Tarzan, except: no abs.

But then, hours after that savory sweet exchange with Mendoza, I'm buzzed out of my sleepy, smiley haze by a text. From Jordan.

He's not checking on me, though. Or circling back on how I'm feeling after my show got canceled. He's not saying he's still sorry about the interview drama, or asking when he's going to see me again. None of that, nope.

He just sent me a link to an article in the *Hollywood Reporter* that says his show just got picked up for season two.

And if you think that's bad (I hope you do; that's bad, right? Like, kind of insensitive?), it's coming in as a group text-chain. With twenty other randos whose numbers I don't even have stored.

"Wow," I say to the stuffed animal I accidentally still sleep with.

But what's funny, if you can call it that, is that gently burned over my corneas is the last self-help quote I was dream-reading, in Heidi's giant book. Like, I'm *seeing* Jordan's article, here in my bedroom, but superimposed above are a bunch of touchy-feely words that I'd only moments before been frolicking around with. And the quote that's lingering says: *Sometimes you have to say goodbye to someone before you can say hello to yourself.*

An actual quote I'd made fun of Aunt Heidi for, back in New York, because she *briefly* considered tattooing the word *goodbye* on one inner wrist, and *hello* on the other. In Chinese. Inspired by this very dopey quote that she came out of the bathroom, reading to me, before I moved back to Jankburg.

"Cool," I recall saying, "I'll, uh, keep that in mind?"

But tonight—or, this morning, actually; it's almost 4:30 a.m.—I sort of see the point of this phrase. I mean, I *really* see it; it's hovering there in my groggy state, floating like debris in a swimming pool that nobody in my part of town could ever afford to maintain.

Sometimes you *do* have to say goodbye to someone before you can say hello to yourself. To your Nate.

Right as Jordan is following up his link with the prayer-sign emoji, which either means "Can't believe I'm this blessed" or "Pray for me, since I'm going to lose so many of you as friends," I switch my phone on airplane mode.

The first time I've ever not responded to a text of his in under fifteen seconds.

And then I roll back over. And hug my own dang self.

And now, bouncing across my inner eyelids, all I see is the faintest etching of the word *Hello*.

The Story of the Day
I Was Born

It's Monday—*Great Expectations* presentation day in English class. And I'm able to see just how overly ambitious my production was.

I see it in the way that McKenna and Kaylee S. deliver their misfire of a *Great Expectations* scene, in which they read one passage from the book, don't even attempt to do British accents, and aren't in period clothing. Mr. English looks pained.

I see it in the way Ethan, Ollie, and Xander present a Keynote slide show called "If *Great Expectations* happened today," an interesting-enough premise except the lead slide spelled "expectations" as "ecspectations," and it never got better from there. Mr. English looks tired.

And ultimately it's my turn, and since I don't have anything formal to present, I just hand Mr. English my "director's notes"—all the observations I pecked into my iPhone as I was taking notes on run-throughs of the show. For Paige to talk louder so they can hear her in the back row, for Jim-Jim to cue the music at a different time.

Bullet points that I added some adjectives to, for Mr. English, because English teachers are obsessed with adjectives. I made the font of my director's notes really big and shrank down the margins and printed it out, and even then it only ended up being two pages. But it is what it is. It's all the gas I've got left in my tank of creativity right now.

I still can't believe a bunch of freakin' lawyers shut down my gymnasium musical.

When the other kids file out of class, Mr. English keeps me, and asks me to read my director's notes out loud. Which is so dumb. But, fine.

And midway through, he cuts me off and looks at me like he's solving a problem, and finally goes, "Fine, I'll give you a B. Look at you, you're on your way to an A."

I click my tongue the way my dad does. "Wait, were you *always* going to give me an A?" My stomach races and my heart gurgles. "Is this just a long, extended metaphor, all our meet-ups and—"

"No. I don't in any way believe every kid starts with an A. I think teachers who say that are liars."

A B. I'll take it. It's better than average but still not perfect. Frankly, a B is very me.

"Ya know, Mr. Foster," Mr. English says, "I taught your dad."

"You did?"

"You bet. I'm old."

In this strange moment it's as if I'm meeting a yeti, or Patti LuPone; somebody epic and unreal. He knew my dad when he was my age?

"What was he like? Like, then, I mean?"

Mr. English smiles and it turns into a yawn. "He was the type of boy who would have given *you* a tough time in the hallways, let's just put it that way."

"People can change," I apparently blurt, and also, apparently, I'm now sticking up for my dad. He gave me his Homecoming suit, ya know? The one he took my mom to, at this very school, in the very gym where I tried to put on my show.

Mr. English holds up my director's notes. "I'm too past my prime and too tired and, frankly, don't care enough to give you a big speech about how you should be applying yourself—how you're inherently brighter and funnier than both your dad and your brother, Anthony, whom I did not teach but whom I do know about, since he's a 'legend' at the school." Mr. English does air-quotes around the word *legend*.

"But let me say: These terribly formatted director's notes show promise. You've got a voice."

"Thanks. Usually people just say I'm loud." Nothing. "That was a *joke* about my voice."

"Right."

He stands, and knocks twice on the two-page director's notes, which I three-hole punched and bound into a black folder, just like how stage managers hand out scripts on Broadway.

"You got out of this town once, Nate," he says. "And that is very impressive. But if you want to get somewhere again, you're going to have to pull your grades up. Way up. All around."

I feel my face do its game-show host impression, eyebrows all surprised, overly smiley smile. "Ahhh, but Mr. English, casting directors don't care about grades."

"Casting directors don't run the world, Mr. Foster."

"They run my world, Mr. English."

A girl from my class pops in and grabs a calculator that she left on her desk, and she says "Sorry" like she's interrupting some kind of important moment.

And that's when I realize maybe it is one.

"You're only a freshman," Mr. English says. "And I want you to graduate this class with a solid A."

I stick out my hand, which does its used-car-salesman impression. "Then it's settled!" I say, "Let's just gimme an A!" all funny. But Mr. English grimaces again.

"Charm can only get you so far."

"As far as New York," I point out, both not unhelpfully and not helpfully.

"I'm going to give you an extra, bonus-points assignment I give my most gifted seniors," he says, and walks over to a tall filing cabinet, straight out of the fifties. He pulls out a photocopy and hands it to me. "Most of the seniors don't finish it because most of them don't quite 'get' it."

The Story of the Day I Was Born," I read, and when I look up, Mr. English's eyes aren't exactly watering but they also aren't not.

"That's easy," I say, confused. "You want a thousand words on the day I was born? I can interview my mom. I mean, my Playbill bio for *E.T.* was fifty words, this can't be that much harder."

Mr. English goes back to his desk and pulls out a metal bell and *dings* it—one of those old-fashioned bells you put at the front desk of a place where you want someone's attention.

"I'm going to ring this every time you're talking when you should be writing."

"But—"

He dings it again, and I shift on my feet, and I

realize my toe hurts and that my shoes are too small now. That I'm growing in real time.

"I don't care about your birthday, not the actual one," he says. "I want to know about the day *you* picked your own birthday."

"I'm lost."

He hovers his hand over the bell, and I close my mouth up like it's a bookbag on the last day of school.

It's quiet for a while.

"Wait, do you mean, like, the day when my life started getting good?"

He smiles and puts the bell back in the drawer.

"Like, the day I count as when I really became myself?"

He half nods, sits back down, and takes out his phone and starts playing with it.

"Can I start the paper with some backstory? Like, about how my parents never recorded me on their home video recorders, but Anthony had *everything* meticulously recorded?"

"Eh." Mr. English waves his hands around like I'm boring him. "Nah. No backstory. Nobody cares about backstory. Overrated. Jump into the good stuff. Free writing tip. Start with an action scene."

I chew the inside of my cheek.

"Well, that's the day I ran away from here. The night, really."

He looks interested, and puts his phone aside but not down. "Okay?"

"My parents were away for the weekend, and Libby found out about the audition for *E.T.*"

He mimes writing with his hand, and when I suppose I look sufficiently confused again, says, "Don't tell me, tell your paper."

"So, wait—you want a paper about the day I ran away to New York?"

"I want you to write yourself out of this place," he says.

"I don't follow."

"I want you to tell the story of how you became the best Nathan Foster possible. Because the key to getting ahead in life, at least in this English class, is to learn how to tell your story in as compelling a way as possible. It's how you'll get scholarships, how you'll get to college, and how you'll ultimately have a satisfying adulthood. Trust me."

I look around the room. "You mean, because *your* life is so satisfying?" I don't mean it to come out sassy. I just don't quite *get* any of this, and why he's being so hard on me.

"No, Mr. Foster. Because my life is not so satisfying. And because I waited too long. This is my last year teaching. Thank God. I wish some adult had told me, a long time ago, what I'm telling you right now.

The only thing that is ultimately interesting about you is your truest story. So, go write it down."

"How long do I have to get the assignment in?"

"However long it takes."

Which could take forever.

I walk out of his classroom, and sort of zombie-strut myself to science, but it's a lab day, so I fake my way through the physical act of pouring some liquid on top of some rock that makes some smoke.

And really what I'm doing is writing my story in my head.

And when I get to lunch, I grab an apple and a string cheese and I break into a music practice room, and open my voice recorder app. And stare at it. And stare at it. And then erase the silent recording and start over.

I decide that maybe he's right. That *my* way to a good grade will be to tell the truth, the whole truth, and (mostly) nothing but the truth. With frequent dance breaks.

"I'd rather not start with any backstory," I say into the voice recorder, and I time-warp myself back to that October evening in my backyard—before Ben, before Jordan, before opening night, before Dad gave me his suit, or Aunt Heidi yelled at me for wandering the streets of New York alone, or before I met a thousand people who believed in me so hard that I somehow ended up believing in myself.

A couple days later and I'm already four chapters into my story, and decide that maybe I'll keep going and not turn it in quite yet. I keep deciding that maybe the story should start later—that I'm getting born all the time. That life is all action scenes if you start thinking about it like it's a novel.

So, I continue voice-recording it, and I start just telling the good parts: the night I first saw two guys kissing in the doorway of a club in New York, and nobody beat them up; the time Anthony took me to Bible camp, and I cried onto Genesis and made the ink bleed.

Mr. English said I could take as long as I needed to tell my story. So I decide to keep telling it till it's finished, whatever my grade ends up being.

Homecoming is in a month. Anthony will be back from Penn State for Thanksgiving. Mom and Dad announced they're going to put in a hammock in the backyard, and Aunt Heidi is coming home for Christmas for the first time in twenty years.

I charge my phone up in anticipation of a lot of voice memos.

When I first came home, I thought high school was going to be straight-up brutal. But mostly, the thing I'm picking up about getting older, and semi-taller, is that all the stuff you think you won't survive ends up being pretty okay. It's the side-swipey junk you don't count on—like, your school cutting the arts program . . . or the first boy you ever kissed, just totally ghosting you—that guts you.

But honestly, that's what best friends and emergency lemon squares are for.

And, yeah, if you're wondering: I erased Jordan's contact info. Because I like Ben more than I love drama. It's sad when stories end, when shows close, and when people leave you. That's . . . a thing that's real and true and sucks about being alive.

But Homecoming is in a month.

And my brother is coming back for Thanksgiving, and secretly makes the best stuffing in the family.

And Mom and Dad, who still fight but recently not quite as often, are putting in a hammock out back. Not that hammocks are inherently romantic, but they're an investment, right? Like, your parents aren't going to put in a hammock and then get divorced, right? So that's something.

And also, Mom said we're going to go to Home Depot to choose the hammock, after Christmas, when they go on sale—and that Ben could come help pick it out too, if he wants. She said it super casual—"Tell that sweet boy Ben to come," she said, "if you want. I like him." If you can believe it. Because I couldn't.

And Aunt Heidi is flying home for Christmas, and we're going to go to *The Nutcracker* downtown, just her and me. And she said we could eat at any restaurant I want. And if there's one theme Aunt Heidi taught me—even before she bought a billion self-help books—it's that, whenever you feel lost, plan your day around meals. Everybody has to eat. So schedule your life and goals around eating times. So logical, but kind of inspired, too.

My stomach rumbles. I want chicken adobo. It's my go-to comfort food now.

I'm only halfway through the first book of my life, which I've decided will cover the crazy period right up until I got hired for *E.T.* That feels like a good birthday, right? Happy Birthday—you're on Broadway, you little weirdo. Ya big doof.

I think I'll call the story of the day I was born

Better Nate Than Ever

Mostly because Mr. English kind of hates puns—and, tough luck for him, you know? This isn't his story, or anyone else's.

It's mine.